Little Book

of Stories

Pat Grieco

Other Books by Pat Grieco

The Art of Nauga Farming

Compulsion

Rhetoric

The Book of Light

Keep the Dance

The Calm Before

Little Book of Stories

Print ISBN: 978-1-7324688-6-3

Pen and Lute
www.penandlute.com

The final approval for this literary material is granted by the author.

Library of Congress Control Number: 2022907806

Distributed Publication
Lexington, KY
Middletown, DE
San Bernardino, CA

Grieco

Little Book of Stories

DEDICATION

For all folk who love stories

Acknowledgement

With gratitude to Sherry
who makes all things possible
and whose patience and thoughtful review
helped make these stories better

Little Book

of Stories

Pat Grieco

I thought I heard a bird today
while sitting on a hill.
It sang, "All cares away, away."
I hear it singing still.

Grieco

CONTENTS

Little Book of Stories

Grieco

In unexpected places

Still life

He sat there, nursing his drink, staring at an old photograph he'd placed on the bar next to his glass. The picture was in good condition for its age, carefully pressed and straightened so that no cracks or smudges would blur the image. It was encased in a fine wood frame underneath what looked like a layer of safety glass. There was an empty spot on the wall behind the bar where it usually hung among other photos and mementos gradually added over the years. That spot was clearly lighter than the rest of the wall which was darkened with age and the accumulated years of smoke and grime.

He'd seen me looking at the picture while I ate my bangers and mash. There was just something about it. The way the three young men gazed back… as though they shared a great secret and were ready to share it with me if only… well if only they were here.

He'd watched me for awhile, then took that picture down from the wall and placed it on the bar. After pulling himself a pint, he sat down on the stool next to me. We sat there quietly for a few minutes, picture in-between us, me with my food, he with his drink. Then, with the fingers of his right hand resting on the wooden frame, he began to speak.

"They were my sons, going off to join the army and fight in the great war. They were boys and young when they left, the sun warm upon their cheeks as they walked away. They were vibrant and full of life and never looked back, so focused as they were on the way ahead.

I have this picture of them here as they were then, eyes bright with visions of adventure, their faces lit by smiles that spoke of happy anticipation of the journey yet to come.

Grieco

It is all I have of them, this picture, to remember them by, frozen in time at the moment of their leaving. They were in a rush to see, to know what lies ahead just around the corner of a life not lived in the straight and narrow confines of a safe, local place. ... Perfect in their youth and eager for adventure, they gave no thought for what they left behind.

It always seems to be that those who stay behind, watching them go, are soon forgotten. I've been told that they lived in frenzied haste, as though there were no tomorrow, reveling in sense and sounds, experiencing each in turn until there were no more to have. Despite the letters I received, I doubt if they lingered long wondering about how things were back home.

The army trained them well and turned them into men and soldiers ready for the fight and enemy to come. And when the fighting came at last, they proved themselves within the fray, ever bold in the face of horrors that those who did return would not speak of.

They survived until the end. And it is one of life's bitter ironies that it was so, that one stray round, with but one day yet to go, should have found them huddled deep within their bunker waiting for the peace to come. I'd like to think they were laughing, sharing some private joke as they were wont to do, just before the shell fell. But I suppose I will never know for sure. Still...

I was told they never knew, that they never felt the impact or the blast that followed quick upon it with death swift and sure as the silence that followed behind.

I have heard it said that it was a blessing that it came so fast, with no warning, fear, or suffering. I have heard it said

3

that it was a tragedy that they should perish then with the end in view.

All I know is that I miss them, bright faced and smiling as the sun shone, the wind blew, and camera captured the memory of them as they were.

They were boys and young when they left..."

He fell silent then and I, not knowing what to say, nodded and said nothing. It seemed enough, for he nodded in return before taking the picture back around the bar and restoring it to its place there on the wall. After carefully straightening it, he paused, as though gathering himself, shook his head, and went back towards the kitchen and out of sight. He did not return, at least as long as I remained which was not long. It was my imagination I know. But I felt the gaze of those boys bearing down upon me as I sat, finishing my meal, in the place where they should be, laughing and sharing a joke with their Da.

I did not linger but left as soon as I scraped the last mash from my plate, leaving behind more cash on the bar than I owed. I felt their gaze, hot upon my back, as I fled the Pub and made my way into the street. Perhaps it was their uniforms, not so very different than mine. Perhaps it was their youth, much like me and my mates. His words haunted me, staying in my mind as I headed to the station and from there back to the regiment. Tomorrow we'd leave for our war, to fight in a land none of us had ever heard of before we'd joined up not so very long ago.

Just like his sons had done, now frozen in time in that picture on the wall behind the bar.

They were boys and young when they left.

In unexpected places

We'd met, as strangers do, in a roadside diner, two people with a need to share each other's burden for a little while. My car was larger than hers and so we took it, with unspoken agreement, out into the countryside, away from prying eyes, to share what comfort each could give.

The mid-day rain brought the sky to darkness. Inside the car, on that isolated road, clarity of vision was not required as her hands moved from my face to the front of my shirt. Some inner sense must have alerted her to some reluctance on my part for she paused, fingers poised upon my chest waiting for some clue on how to proceed.

"What's the matter Hun?" She said in the darkness as the rain beat down upon my rental car. I sighed and shrugged my shoulders, the motion somewhat lost in the car's dim interior.

"I don't know. I guess I'm just dissatisfied with my life. I hate my job. I've got a lousy two-bit apartment. Night classes are killing me. I don't get enough sleep and I'm here in the middle of nowhere trying to make some sense out of it all. Trying to find some meaning, some connection that'll make it all worthwhile. … I guess you could say… I'm unhappy." I shrugged my shoulder again. "Yeah. That's it. I'm unhappy."

She snorted just a little, suppressing a larger laugh.

"Hun, Happiness is what happens while you're doing something else. Don't look for it, 'cause you won't find it."

She leaned back against the door, resting her head on the window.

"Oh there'll be moments. They sneak up on you when you're not expecting them. It'll be the small things; a kid's grin, a lover's kiss, the sun breaking out on a rainy day. It'll hit you smack between the eyes, and you'll realize that for that one moment, that one instant, you're happy, and it's good to be alive, good to be you, you belong, and you wouldn't want to be anywhere else in the world."

She laughed softly, "Of course, the moment ends as quick as it came and you're back in the thick of things, fighting and struggling to keep your head above water. Sometimes the moments last longer than others, but they all end. Take me... big house, rich husband, four kids, all the clothes and fine things I could ever want... but in the end I'm here with you in the rain on some godforsaken backroad in this rental car trying to find some magic, searching for heat in a cold world, looking for solace when each drop of rain marks another second less in this miserable existence."

"What happened?"

"He left me for a younger woman."

She smiled and it was easy to see, even in the dark, the beauty clinging to her even now.

"Said she made him happy."

She laughed again, a slightly bitter sound mixed in.

"Happy. Shit! I'd given him four kids, hosted his dinner parties, nursed him when he was sick, stood by him through all the lean years, and he had the gall to tell me she made him happy!"

Grieco

She left the word hanging there like an epithet... and perhaps it was.

"Made me mad as Hell. Made me want to strip that bastard of everything he'd ever owned. Made me realize that everything I had, every possession I'd gathered was all I'd take out of the relationship. Made me understand that nothing is permanent, that the only thing that matters is the here and now, to live today because tomorrow holds no promise past a fool's dream, ... that the only sure thing is what you have, right now, this moment, this feeling, this emotion, this connection."

She leaned forward and kissed me, slowly lingering as her hands moved gently, mussing my hair and finally resting on my chest, fingering the buttons on my shirt.

"He took everything I thought I had, everything I thought I wanted. Shit... everything I thought I needed."

She laughed again and looked me straight in the eyes as she moved her hands downward.

"But he never made me unhappy. You have to do that to yourself, have to wallow in self-pity, denial, and fear of losing what you have instead of embracing what awaits. Hun, if you live in the moment, you can't possibly be unhappy. You're too busy living to even notice one way or the other."

Just then, the sun broke through the clouds, splaying light across the car's interior, revealing her trim, unclad body. And whether it was her words, her kiss, or the slow magic of her touch, I began to think she might just be right.

The Hitman

He was perfectly average in appearance; average height, average build, average facial features, and was dressed in a nondescript way that would blend in just about anywhere.

In fact, no one was likely to give him a second look or maybe even notice him at all. And that was the point. It allowed him to go places and do things someone more remarkable couldn't. It made him invisible in the normal course of things, just another face in the crowd, one of a million nondescript people passing by unnoticed every day.

And that, in a way, made it possible for him to be where he was today, kneeling next to someone lying crumpled at the bottom of the second-floor landing of a stairwell in an apartment building just far enough off the beaten path to be the ideal location for meetups one might not want others to be aware of.

Feeling for a pulse, he nodded as if finding one was what he had expected, indeed had hoped for. Then, he spoke gently, almost solicitously to the motionless figure whose eyes were fixed on his in an urgent, desperate, silent plea for help.

"I have always been misunderstood. It is not so much that I enjoy killing. It is simply that I have always been so good at it. It is a source of pride, much as any craftsman would find in his work.

It is the little things, the mastery of which makes the approach, the blending in with expectations, so rewarding. Taking the target unawares even when the hunt was expected, perhaps even known, is… exquisite. The sense of accomplishment is complete when you can look the target in the eye and know, know that they truly do not see you, that you have become as much a part of the surroundings as a tree, a dog, or any of the thousands of inconsequential persons noticed but unobserved.

Unlike some, I do not torture my victims. I do not delight in the unnecessary infliction of pain or suffering. I could, I suppose, if it was required. But it all seems trite somehow, the killer having somehow trapped the prey, letting it linger while terror unhinges every fiber of existence.

I prefer to catch the target unaware, in the act of living, of enjoyment, in the fullness of the moment, so that the last thought, the last experience is of happiness, of contentment, and a sense of rightness in the world. They're dead before they have a chance to know otherwise. Before the shock of pain, of injury, can mar the perfection of the moment, can ruin the beauty captured in that last breath when tomorrow is an expectation, a known, a certainty no more.

There's a certain creativity to it. I like to make each experience unique, completely, or at least somewhat different than the others. Anyone can shoot someone from across the street. But it takes an artist to integrate oneself into the target's life, on a level which gives access yet makes one secondary to the target's world and interests.

It is sad in a way to be part of someone's everyday life and to go unnoticed, to be as a tree or a rock and yet go unseen… ever there, always present yet ignored in the face of more important things. And yet, that makes the end somehow sweeter when the tree limb falls, when the rock trips them, and nature itself provides closure, no longer silent background to target's fate.

Little Book of Stories

Tricky that, to make nature an accomplice in the deed, but it can be done with subtle ministrations to ease the way. A weakened limb, a raised or loosened rock, can be the very thing to set events in motion toward a certain end. A fall is just a fall until it is not, and nearby help may be a fatal guide to the fallen's fate.

Anything can be a weapon, anything an instrument for accident if timing, if circumstance should allow. A pen within a pocket may pierce the heart if chance provides the method for misfortune to occur. A neck may break on misstep on a rocky path or tumble from a horse gone momentarily mad from biting fly, a burr, or snake upon the path.

All, all, are unexpected. All provide a chance, a hope that all will be well, and life will continue as before. And if it should, well who's to say that that is not as it should be? Certainly not I. An artist does not question the outcome or the fashion of the work. It becomes what it must. It finds its final form with artist but observer to the piece now complete and beyond the right to intervene.

But you may ask, 'How do I choose my victims?' If truth be told, I do it for pay. Even an artist needs to make a living after all. But they chose themselves sometimes, through deed, through chance, through fate.

Take you for instance. You were abusive to your wife and son in the shopping mall. That was enough to gain my interest. Once I checked further, the incidents of domestic violence, your roughshod manner and disdain for your co-workers and those you supervised, and the embezzlement you worked so hard to hide, those, those got my full attention. And when I found out about the affairs, all of them, well that settled it. You were my boy. All that remained was to devise the method, the timing, and the nature of the "accident" that would claim you in such an unexpected fashion.

What? How much to do all this? There's usually a fixed basic fee with a sliding scale based on the target's importance and level of difficulty. But for you? Nothing. Absolutely nothing. You were a freebie, all on me. I considered this a gift to humanity and by the way to your wife and children. The insurance and the Cayman accounts should keep them more than comfortable. And don't worry, I know someone who can be trusted to help manage their affairs. Well… maybe I did keep something for myself. I did keep the Swiss account for my trouble, but in the scheme of things those five million Euros were a trifling sum compared to the rest of your estate.

Shhhh. Don't try to speak. It will all be over soon." He paused for just a moment, leaning back on his heels as he watched all hope slowly fade from the prone figure's eyes. "… You know, in a strange way, I almost feel like I should thank you. .. I don't often have a chance to talk about my work this way. You have been a most … receptive listener."

He leaned forward once more, resting his hands just below the motionless figure's neck. "It's almost a shame that we must end this chat." He glanced briefly towards the stairs leading down to the first floor. "Regrettably however, your current dalliance should be coming up those stairs in about fifteen minutes. I imagine she will be quite distressed to find that you somehow slipped and fell, breaking your neck in the process.

I could leave you here like this, paralyzed, unable to talk. No one would be the wiser. You'd surely never tell and the torture of having to be kept alive by machines and feeding tubes would certainly be a fitting punishment. But then your wife would be saddled with you and denied the happier life that this accident makes possible." He paused once more, as if thinking through the possibilities, the choices. Then he shook his head and smiled, almost apologetically, before continuing. "No. No. I think it's better that you just slip away peacefully as a result of this most tragic accident.

Don't worry. You won't feel a thing. Just a simple twist to finish what the fall began, and we'll be done here. Ready? Close your eyes. It will be easier on you. No? Very well. Here we go. One, two... there... all done.

And now just down the stairs and out into the night and I am gone..."

And he was. But first, he gently patted the face of the recently deceased, then leaned back and stood, casually adjusting his clothing before descending to the first floor and making his way out the building's entrance. Once outside, he just walked away, blending and disappearing amongst the people passing by. No one noticed, or, if they did, bothered to give him a second glance. He was, after all, just an average man among all the other average folk, and no one to be concerned about.

Chance encounter

Two folk stood in the exhibit hall of the museum, gazing at the beautifully preserved trunk of a rare and ancient tree. The creator of the exhibit beamed with pride as the other marveled at the display.

"What a magnificent specimen!"

"Yes, it is. We were lucky to come across it."

"You found it by chance?"

"Oh sure. We were looking for a completely different tree when we came around a set of boulders and there it was."

"It must have been really special to see it out there in the wild."

"It was. We couldn't believe our eyes. It stood there against the sky, majestic and beautiful. It looked incredibly ancient."

"How old was it."

"4,900 years, give or take a few one way or the other. You don't find many trees still alive after all that time."

"Wow! That must have been maybe the oldest tree in the world."

"Yeah, well we thought that it was just that at the time."

"How did you determine its age?"

Little Book of Stories

"We counted the rings from a cross section of its trunk. You can only imagine how long that took. Had to do it three times for accuracy. Can't be too careful with that sort of thing."

"I can only imagine. ... Wait, you said that the tree was alive when you found it."

"Yep. Magnificent sight."

"So how did it end up here, in the museum?"

"Well... we cut it down."

"You cut it down?"

"Yep. "

"Uh... why?"

"Had to. It was the only way to find out for sure just how old it was."

"the only way..."

"Yep. We tried to core it but the drill bit broke. The only other way we had was to cut that sucker down and count the rings."

"So let me see if I understand. ... You found the tree by a chance encounter..."

"Yep."

"It was alive when you found it..."

Grieco

"Yep."

"You thought it looked pretty old and wanted to figure out how old it really was…"

'Yep."

So you cut it down in order to count the rings…"

"Yep."

"In other words you killed the oldest tree in the world so you could figure out how old it was."

"Yep. Had to. There was no other way to figure it out. Sure is a magnificent specimen though, isn't it…"

A Pebble

He was the best-looking dead man I had ever seen. Sunday suit, gentle smile, hands resting lightly on his still stomach as he lay there within his padded box.

It was not at all as I had seen him last, sitting on the sidewalk in the cold October rain, coughing up a lung with deep, throaty sounds wet with phlegm and thick from cigarettes and hooch.

He'd sat there, huddled under plastic poncho, wearing a thick, green, hooded sweatshirt he'd found somewhere, now stained and dirty from months of wear, and trousers, of some indistinguishable shade of gray, and boots, that only matched in the degree of wear shown by each.

"Move out of the rain. You'll catch your death."

"I'm dead already." he'd replied. "Or as good as. TB."

He'd coughed again. This time spewing gobs of red tinged phlegm into the torn and ratty T-shirt he'd use to cover his mouth. When he could breathe again, he continued, gesturing with the rain-soaked cloth.

"Yea, I'm dead already but I'd rather be dead out here, in the open being washed clean than in some dark, flea-bitten shelter. A man can face himself outside and know himself for what he is."

He'd nodded to himself, rain dripping from the poncho's hood.

Grieco

"You can think. You can see it all right here, and here, and here." he said pointing to his head, and chest, and ragged cloth clutched in his left hand.

"I'm dead Ben. And I'm not afraid of that. I was always more afraid of life than of death, of being hurt, hurt in every way a man can be, that I shut myself away in books, in religion, in booze, 'til I wasn't a man at all, just some shadow in the sun, a spot upon a bright world of motion, noise, and realness.

Shoot. I was a Doctor." He laughed, short and quick. "A Doctor for Christ sake. I knew what I was doing. Knew I was out of touch with everything that mattered, but I was scared, too scared I'd fail, too scared I'd disappoint others, too scared I'd succeed and be expected to be more than I was, of what I knew myself to be… a sham, an imposter, a man in a white coat pretending to heal others when he couldn't even heal himself."

He spasmed for a moment as he fought for control then cleared his throat and spat a gob of green upon the ground where the rain worked at it awhile.

"I'm dead Ben, but I'm more alive now than when I had a job, a wife, a life, and all the little things that came with it."

He coughed, more violently this time, body wracked with the effort and when he stopped, he leaned back against the building wall, eyes closed as the rain washed down his face, so many tears for the wasted years.

"Ben." he said weakly. "It was only after I ended here, after I died, that I understood what living was. All I ever had to do was be, just be, like a pebble in a stream, immersed in the water, moved by it, but always a pebble, never a stone, never the water.

I could have been me, not someone else's version, not someone else's expectation, not even my own… simply a pebble."

He opened his eyes briefly to look tiredly, searchingly at me.

"Do you understand Ben? Do you know what I'm telling you?"

I sighed and shook my head.

"No Tom. I don't. All I know is that it's cold and wet and I need to get you inside and looked after."

Tom laughed, as if genuinely amused.

"Too late Ben." he'd said. "Too late for that."

He seemed to settle into himself, sinking beneath the surface. He opened one eye, took a ragged breath and softly said, "You'll see Ben. You'll understand… when it's time."

He smiled then, almost like the one he wore now, warm and dry in his box, whispered almost too low for me to hear, "A pebble…", and was gone.

"I'll bury you tomorrow, Tom, but I don't understand, won't pretend that I do. I don't even agree with what you said.

Goddamn it Tom! We're not pebbles. We're not some helpless piece of stone mired in some rushing stream.

Grieco

We can act. We can choose. We can even change the stream if we're bold enough and smart enough and strong enough.

Tom. You were my brother. You should have known better. You should have been better, should have fought longer, shouldn't have died on some godforsaken sidewalk, a stranger to all who passed except for me, who found you too late, after you were washed clean, after you had surrendered yourself, after you had become a pebble."

He was the best-looking dead man I had ever seen…

Message

"Want to leave a message?"

I paused. What kind of message do you leave after ten years for the one who broke your heart? One minute I was happy, the next shattered as our life, our love was held up as the lie it was.

Suspended in time, on one knee, ring in hand, surrounded by hushed and curious onlookers in the mood lit restaurant, I had waited for her answer. An eternity, it seemed like an eternity, and then she smiled, put her hand to her lips as she took a deep breath and slowly let it out.

"I love you." she said, and my heart soared with the sureness of her next words. "But…" My heart stopped… and time slowed to a standstill as I knelt, frozen, waiting for the next words to fall upon my hopes.

"I can't…" and there it was, the rock to break my dreams to splendid shards, bright but scattered reflections of a future now not to be.

"I can't leave my mother. Especially now, and…" She paused, tears welling in her eyes. "… you're leaving, going overseas…"

"She could come with us, live with us." knowing as I said it, I was grasping at straws, hoping for the words to change and her answer to be different.

"No. Mom will never leave while he's still alive, while there's still a chance he'll pull through."

Grieco

"Sus..." She put her fingers to my lips to stop me from saying what we both knew. That the accident was fatal, that the fact that he had survived this long was a miracle but that, in the end, no matter how long he lingered, drifting in and out of awareness, he was a dead man. It was just a matter of time, today, tomorrow, or a year from now.

"I understand." I heard myself saying as I put the ring away, pulled myself back to my chair and took a long swallow of the wine that had been a favorite 'til then.

"I'm sorry." She said, tears falling slowly to darken the patterned table covering. I nodded, mute, unable to trust myself to speak. I don't remember much more of that evening except that we finished dessert in awkward silence that stretched through the drive back and the soft, sweet kiss that marked goodbye with unlooked for finality.

I left the next morning, taking my assignment early. I hadn't talked to her since. It was only much later that I'd learned she was expecting, and still longer still that she had had twins, girls... apparently favoring their mother. Her Dad had lingered in that twilight state for six years before finally letting go. I sent flowers and a card from Algiers but kept myself buried in endless days of paperwork and management of projects whose main redeeming value was they helped me forget. Helped me move from one day to the next in a semblance of living.

I'd been back in New York for a year when I heard, and I knew I had to go. Knew I'd never forgive myself if I didn't. So here I was, standing on the doorstep, eyes downcast, turning my hat in my hands, as her mother said, "Want to leave a message?"

"Tell her..." I paused, my eyes resting on a face so much like hers, except the eyes were blue, not green and it wore the burden of twenty more years of life.

"Tell her I heard about the accident..." a terrible crash, just like her father's, on ice on a backroad. She had lain trapped for three days at the bottom of a ravine, mangled car a cocoon, pressing tight against the wounds that would have killed her otherwise. A hiker had found her, and it had taken another twelve hours to cut her free and move her to the trauma center where she had been these last ten days. "that I came by to see... to help."

She studied me for a moment, then seemed to come to a decision. "The monthly checks have helped a lot." I nodded in mute acknowledgement. "She'd keep the envelopes you know... postmarked from around the world. ... She always knew where you were and read about the places and the things. ... It kept her connected to you."

I just stared. "I never..."

"Of course not. How could you? ... Though you could have called you know." Her eyes locked with mine and didn't let go. "She never gave up on you. She waited, waited for you to come to your senses, to get over... well... you know..."

I waved my hat vaguely as I replied. "She made her decis..."

Her snort broke me off in mid word. "We all make decisions, ones we're not always happy with afterwards. I've always known the price she paid to stay with me. I can only imagine the price you've paid to stay away."

Grieco

I looked down, somehow embarrassed by it all. "The girls, are they... were they..."

She smiled for the first time and her strain seemed to lessen just a bit. "They're fine. They were with me that day. They're worried. They love their mother and I've done my best to reassure them... to tell them it will be all right."

"And will it?" I gazed at her face, trying hard to gauge the truth, in her eyes, in the set of her jaw as she replied.

"Yes. She'll be fine. The doctors say she'll need home care for some time, but they expect a full recovery."

A lie, was it a lie or was that my fear speaking? She had told us much the same when her husband had come home, pale and weak, from the hospital. How could I trust her now?

"Would you like to see the twins? They're taking a nap. It's been a long week for them, but we could look in on them for a minute."

I hesitated, knowing once through that door I would never truly leave again. "I..."

She stepped down and took me by the arm. "Come on, you should see them." she encouraged gently and led me to the door. I hesitated as she opened it and began to step through. "They have your eyes you know." and in that instant I was caught, snared in all the hopes long lost and dreams left scattered on that restaurant floor so many years before.

She smiled once more, as though understanding, and went inside. And despite myself, I followed.

Sallie doesn't work here anymore

The newsroom was unusually quiet for a Tuesday. Many desks were empty, and the overall atmosphere was subdued, almost as though the entire office was holding its breath, waiting for ... something ... to happen. Without warning, the brooding silence was broken when one of the few people there reacted enthusiastically to the sight of a co-worker coming through the newsroom doors.

"Jim! Welcome back! How was the vacation?"

"Good. Amazing how fast thirty days goes by."

"I can only imagine. Someday I'll have to try it. But to bring you up to speed... things have changed a little bit since you've been gone."

"How so?"

"Well... You remember how we were bought last year?"

"Sure. Big media conglomerate. Owners said they wanted to expand their market share by buying a respected, independent media voice. Hands off folks. Said they wouldn't interfere in how things were run."

"Well, they've changed their minds. Decided to get more involved after all in the day to day running of things."

"Huh! Didn't expect that. Thought they'd more or less honor what they told folks going into the deal. ... I noticed that Sallie's name wasn't on the sign out front. She get promoted?"

"Sallie doesn't work here anymore..."

Grieco

"What? How? When?"

"Happened shortly after you left. Owners came in and had a big meeting. Said they wanted to take things in a new direction. Laid out their vision for revising the ways things got done.

Everybody listened. Some folks even nodded. Most folks just looked at each other like those guys were speaking Greek. Just didn't seem to make much sense based on what this place stands for."

"Well, we always thought that the new guys would want to make some changes. Put their own spin on things..."

"Yeah. But not like this. Not to this extent. Not to this extreme."

"How bad could it be?"

"Bad... Started by bringing Sallie in for a meet. Said they respected all the work she'd done as Managing Editor, but it was time for a change. Gave her a bonus as part of her severance package and politely kicked her out the door."

"But she was the heart of this place. She set the tone for everything we do here. She heads... headed the editorial board... Had her fingers in everything..."

"Yep. But she's gone. New guy started last week. Already made big changes. A lot of folks have been let go."

"Ben?"

"Didn't like his politics."

"Mary?"

"Thought her views were in opposition to their own."

"Charlie?"

"Well they offered him a position. But in the end, he couldn't get himself to sacrifice his principles... Left last week."

"Tom? Pete? Bill? Larry? Mort?"

"All gone. They just didn't fit in with how the new bosses wanted to do things, how they wanted us to report, the viewpoint they want this institution to espouse..."

"Well then why the heck am I here? I'm much more radical than Mary ever was. I pull no punches in my writing. I don't do fluff pieces and I sure as hell don't agree with the direction these guys seem to be taking us in."

"You're the token."

"The token?"

"Yeah. The guy they can hold up to prove that they entertain every side of an issue... that they're fair and balanced even though they champion only one point of view... targeted and tailored for a specific audience."

"Well hell... just hell. What exactly am I supposed to do now? They know I can't just walk out on my contract. ... I've got a family to support... bills to pay. ... Julie's just got into braces for Christ sake."

Grieco

"I don't know what to tell you. … At least you'll have a job... maybe be able to make a difference if they give you enough slack in the reins to do what you want."

"I wish Sallie was here. She'd know what to do. She was a rock… the center of this newsroom."

"Yeah… she was. But Sallie doesn't work here anymore.

Fishing Trip

The three of us waited near the water, gear in hand, ready to begin. We had gotten there in my grandfather's old blue Camino which he sometimes let my older brother drive. Sitting in grandfather's lap, my brother would hold the wheel of that beat-up thing, grinning like this was the essence of his dreams. But we were past that now. Now, now we stood on the rocky bank of a swiftly running stream, flush with the excitement of what lay ahead.

We waited there, water rushing by, as we readied ourselves for the challenge yet to come. The Brookies were running, a phrase that conjured up all sorts of images to a small boy's mind. To be sure, they were fish of a kind I do not understand even now. But it was an adventure that day, an expedition with my grandfather and older brother, a chance to meet nature at its finest and achieve victory, small though it might be. And so we stood there, poles and net in hand until, with a smile, a laugh, and the quiet urging of that grand old man, we began to fish.

I say fish though with the small creatures flowing past in their thousands it was something less than that. It took no skill to hook or net them by the dozens, even for we boys who lacked even the most basic knowledge of the ways of fish. But it was exciting and gratifying in its way to capture what Nature was offering us and others that day.

We got wet. We got cold. We braved the dangers of the current and the rushing stream, but we endured until, after several hours, we had caught our fill, packed our rods and net and catch, and left for home.

I have not been back since, though I pass that same spot from time to time. And when I do, I cannot help but think about that day so long ago, vanished in the long-lost past. It is not as clear now as it was then, when we were steeped in youth and fresh from our adventure. But I remember it still and the steady hands that kept an overeager boy from slipping off the rocks into the rushing water just below.

It is not my only memory of my grandfather, but it is a sure and certain one that I return to on a day like this, gray and drizzly, in the short time before the onslaught of Winter. He has been gone now for some fifty years and more, but, in my mind, he remains here at this spot sharing with two small boys the essence of adventure and the joy of life.

I am far, far from that simple fishing trip with the tricks of time making me different than I was, there, standing on that rocky bank. But I still see us as we were, caught up in that moment of adventure, where nothing else existed but the swiftly moving water, the fish, and the three of us. And dreary day or not, it shall ever be so.

Traffic Stop

*It happens to all of us at some point or another. The red
and blue lights suddenly start to flash in the rear-view
mirror. Perhaps the sound of a police siren can be heard,
and all that's left is to pull over to the side of the road and
wait for the cop to make their way up to the driver's
window. Today, it's the turn of a light blue SUV. A young
woman, named Susie, sits behind the wheel, with her sister,
Sarah, in the front passenger seat. Both wait nervously as
the officer approaches.*

"Good evening, Ma'am. License and registration please."

"Ah… certainly officer. Is there a problem?"

"No ma'am. Not necessarily. Just a standard safety check
for every vehicle traveling within twenty miles of the
border."

"Safey check?"

"Yes ma'am. The law passed by the legislature, just last
week, mandates that all vehicles within twenty miles of the
state line be inspected for safety. … Could you open the
hatch ma'am?"

"I don't understand. Why would you need…"

"Just open the hatch ma'am."

"Ah… ok." Susie pushes a button on her key fob and the
rear hatch door opens.

"Thank you, ma'am. This should only take a moment." The
officer goes to the rear of the car and sorts through some

bags, clothes, and assorted items, then pushes them aside and opens the spare tire compartment. After peering inside, he closes the compartment and then the hatch door and walks back up to the driver's side window. He hands the license and registration back to the driver. "Well, everything seems in order. ... Where are you folks headed?"

"We're on our way to see our mother."

"She live out of state?"

"Yes sir. About two hours from here. We hope to get there by supper. She makes the best chicken fried steak with all the fixings, and we hope to get there in time to help out."

"I see." The officer pauses for a moment before continuing. "Well then ma'am, there is one more thing before I let you go. ..."

"There is?"

"Yes ma'am. Let me see your period card."

"Why of course, sir." Susie reaches for her purse and takes out what appears to be a small calendar with markings in red ink on it.

The officer takes it and looks at it briefly, then leans in towards the window and addresses Sarah. "You too ma'am. I need to see your period card please."

Sarah looks startled and confused. "I'm sorry officer. I don't know what that is."

Susie interrupts before the officer can say anything more. "My sister is from New York, officer. She's only visiting. They don't require their woman to have period cards up there."

The officer looked from Susie to Sarah. "That right ma'am? You from New York?"

"Yes sir."

"Do you have some ID? Something to prove that?"

"Why, yes sir. I do. Here's my driver's license."

The officer takes the license and looks it over, turning it to exam both sides. Then, apparently satisfied, he hands it back to Sarah. "Thank you, ma'am. I understand that you're from out of state, but according to the new law, that doesn't matter. You have to carry a period card with you at all times."

Sarah is clearly taken aback by this. "But I don't have one. I just flew in so we could travel together to visit our mother…"

The officer looks somewhat apologetic. "I understand, ma'am. However, it is the law hereabouts. You have to have one."

"Well I don't and there isn't much chance for me to get one before we leave the state."

The officer pauses at that, takes off his hat and rubs his head before pulling his hat back on. "Well, … there is one other thing we can do since you don't have a card."

Grieco

Brightening somewhat at this, Sarah looks up from putting her license back in her purse. "And what is that officer?"

"You'll have to take a pregnancy test."

Both sisters react to this. "What!"

The officer, one hand on the doorframe, bends down some to gain a better view of the interior of the car. He looks from one sister to the other and then addresses Susie. "You too ma'am. Your card shows you haven't had a period for six weeks or so."

She looks at him, hard and steady. "And what business is that to you? A lot of women have variable periods. They don't always happen like clockwork you know."

The officer has the good grace to look somewhat embarrassed. "Yes ma'am. I suppose that's true. However, the law states that no pregnant woman will be allowed to cross state lines. It's a felony for them to do so. So ... if you'd be so kind as to step out of the car..."

The women do so. Susie puts the car keys in her purse and then turns towards him. "What now officer?"

"If you'll wait right there, I'll go get the tests and privacy screen from my patrol car." He turns and walks the few feet to his vehicle. After opening the trunk, he takes out a box that looks much like a first aid kit and places it on the ground. Then he moves a few things around and pulls out something that looks a little like a folded lawn chair. However, as he opens it up, it becomes apparent that it's a cloth screen mounted on a metal frame. He sets that up at the rear of the patrol car and then returns to the women, kit in hand. He places the kit on the ground and opens it. He takes out two sealed pregnancy tests, closes the kit, and hands one test to each woman. "Alright then. I'll need you, one at a time, to go behind that screen and pee on those tests."

Both women take the proffered tests but Sarah, clearly indignant, opens her mouth to speak. Before she can, her sister stops her, placing a hand on her arm. "Of course, officer. I'll go first, shall I?"

"That's fine ma'am. Just hand over your purse please."

"And why is that officer?"

"Can't run the chance of a test being adulterated or faked ma'am." He gestures with his hand. "Your purse ma'am."

Susie hands him her purse and starts to walk past him towards the patrol car. The officer holds out his hand to stop here. "Ah… just a moment ma'am."

"Is there something else officer?"

"Yes ma'am, there is. Please put your hands on the patrol car. I'm required to search your person to make sure you haven't got anything hidden on you that would help you fake the test."

Susie sighs, clearly exasperated by this whole business. "Is that really necessary officer?"

"Yes ma'am, I'm afraid so. … Now put your hands on the car please."

Susie does so, leaning somewhat forward and supporting the weight of her body on her hands. The officer does a thorough, invasive search, leaving nothing to chance. Finally he finishes, apparently satisfied that she's not hiding anything. "Alright ma'am, you can step behind the screen now. ... But no funny business."

Susie, her face showing a mix of outrage and mortification, does so. In the space between the ground and the bottom of the screen, you can see one foot lift and then the other as she takes off her panty. A moment later her voice can be heard. "Ah officer?"

"Yes ma'am?"

"You want me to pee on the test, correct?"

"Yes ma'am."

"Should I just pee on the side of the road or is there something for me to pee into?"

"The side of the road is fine ma'am."

A loud sigh from behind the screen is followed by the sound of a stream of liquid hitting the pavement. Susie's voice can be heard a moment later. "Officer... you wouldn't happen to have some tissues to ah... clean myself up with, would you?"

The officer is clearly embarrassed by this turn of events. "Ah... yes ma'am. Absolutely ma'am. If you just look in the trunk right there, you'll see a couple of boxes with tissues and cleaning cloths." He paused for a moment. "Are you finding them alright?"

"Yes officer. I found them. I'll be finished in a minute."

Little Book of Stories

"Take your time ma'am."

Sarah and the officer wait silently for a few minutes while Susie cleans up. Finally, she comes back around the screen, walks over to the officer, and hands him the test. She seems barely able to contain her anger at what she's just had to do. "Is there anything else you need officer? An ultrasound perhaps… a note from my doctor…"

The officer gives Susie her purse back and then puts the test in a baggie and the baggie into a pocket in his uniform. "Ah… no ma'am. Now we just have to wait a few minutes for the results." He turns to Sarah. "Now ma'am, if you'd be so kind…" He motions for her to "assume the position" on the patrol car.

Sarah doesn't move from where she's standing. Instead, she holds up her right hand in a gesture meant to stop anything else the officer might say. "Let me save both of us some time and trouble. … I'm eight weeks pregnant."

Susie turns towards Sarah, obviously surprised by her statement. "Sarah! Is it true? That's wonderful news! How long have you known? How did Mark react?" She rushes over to Sarah and hugs her.

Sarah returns the hug. Then as they separate, she says, "I've only known for a week. I'd been feeling… different for some time now, and then, when I missed my period, I got a test from the drugstore. Even then, I couldn't really believe that I might be pregnant, so I put off taking it for awhile until I got my nerve up. … Mark doesn't know yet. He's been away on a business trip to Asia and won't be back for another week at least. I'm going to tell him then. Didn't seem right to do it over the phone."

Grieco

Susie holds her at arm's length, seemingly reluctant to let her go. "No. No. Of course not. But still. This is fantastic news. You and Mark will make wonderful parents."

At this point, the officer shifts some, rocking back and forth on his feet, and clears his throat. "Ah hem…" causing the women to turn their attention back to him. "Um… Congratulations ma'am. That's good news. I'm sure your husband will be delighted to hear all about it." He takes the unused test from Sarah and puts it back into the kit. Then he takes Susie's test out of his pocket. "All that's left then is to see how this one turned out." He peers at the test strip, examining it closely. "Two lines… Well, it seems like congratulations are in order for you as well ma'am. You're also pregnant."

Susie stands still for a moment, clearly shocked by the result. "That… that can't be. I'm on the pill. Jack and I aren't ready for a baby. We're waiting until we can afford it and with my hypertension…"

It's Sarah's turn to hug her sister. "I'm sure everything will turn out ok Susie. Jack will jump for joy when he hears the news… and they're doing great things with hypertension these days. I'm sure your pregnancy will be just fine."

Susie holds on to her sister for a while longer. Then, recovering somewhat from the shock of finding out she's pregnant, turns back to the officer. "Well then, I guess we're done here. Just two pregnant sisters on the way to have dinner with their mother. Nothing unusual about that." She takes Sarah by the elbow and turns away, starting to move back towards their car, only to be stopped by the officer.

"I'm sorry ma'am, but I can't let you leave."

Susie turns back to the officer, her indignation clearly visible. "And why not?... Haven't you done enough today, invading our privacy, subjecting me to a body search, making me stand behind that screen. ... You have no right..."

"I'm sorry ma'am but I do. The law requires me to do everything I've done today."

"Well it can't stop us from going to our mother's."

"Yes ma'am, it can. ... You did say that she lives out of state?"

Susie pauses, the implications beginning to sink in. "Yes. About two hours from here."

The officer nods, somewhat sympathetically. "I see. ... Well then ma'am, I can't let you visit your mom. State law prohibits it now that you're pregnant."

"It prohibits us from seeing our mother?"

"Not exactly ma'am. ... It prohibits any pregnant woman from leaving the state as a measure to prevent them from traveling to get an abortion. If a woman were to do that, at any time after conception, the law says that she and those who helped are guilty of murder. Since folks can't be trusted not to try anyway, the best way to prevent that is to stop them from leaving the state. And since your mom lives out of state, that means you won't be able to see her today."

Susie reaches into her purse, takes out the car keys and gives them to her sister. "Then you go Sarah. Tell mother what happened here. ... I'll call an Uber and go home."

Grieco

Sarah looks her sister, dismayed at what's just happened. "But Susie…"

"Just go!"

Sarah reluctantly begins to turn away when the voice of the officer stops her. "I'm sorry ma'am, but you can't go either."

Susie turns to the officer, eyes blazing with anger. "But why? She's not from here. She's from New York. For God's sake, she just flew in today. The law can't apply to her."

The officer nods, almost condescendingly. "I can understand your confusion ma'am, but the law makes no exceptions. It don't matter if you're from out of state or not. If you're pregnant, you can't cross the state line. It's a felony to do so, pure and simple. As I said, … no exceptions."

Susie's face becomes a mask of calm, hiding the anger seething within. She responds in a very reasonable tone of voice. "Ah… well thank you for clearing that up officer. I guess we'll just have to make that trip another time then." She turns to Sarah. "Shall we go then? We can give mother a call on the way home and explain why we can't make it today." They both turn and again begin to move towards their car.

The officer stops them again. "I can't let you do that ma'am. There's no way to tell that you won't just take some back road and try to cross the border someplace else."

Little Book of Stories

Susie looks him in the eye while gently nudging her sister to keep her moving towards the car. "Can't you just trust us officer? I give you my word that we'll go straight home."

The officer smiles. "I might even believe you ma'am. But once you get back in that car there's just no way for me to be sure now, is there?"

With a final push, Susie urges Sarah towards the car. "Go now! Run!"

The officer pulls a taser from a holster at the side of his belt. "Stop! Stop or I'll taser you!"

"Keep going!" Susie yells and turns to run towards the car.

The officer fires the taser, hitting Susie in the back. She jerks. Her momentum carries her forward a bit before she falls to the ground. Sarah stops at this and moves to her sister's side. "Susie! Susie!" She turns to the officer. "What did you do?!"

The officer takes a long white zip tie from some hanging at his belt. He turns Susie over and fastens it around her wrists, securing it by pulling it tight. "My job ma'am." He turns to look at Sarah. "Now I'm not going to have any trouble with you, am I ma'am?" Sarah just stares at him, dumbfounded by events. "Hold out your hands, ma'am." Sarah does so and the officer takes another zip tie and fastens it around her wrists. The officer takes hold of one of Susie's arms and starts to help her up as she begins to recover from the taser. "Now help me get your sister over to the patrol car." He looks at Sarah as she continues to just sit there. "Please."

Grieco

The officer gets them over to the patrol car, opens the back door and helps a still dazed Susie get in, making sure she doesn't hit her head as she does so. Then, after closing the door, he leads Sarah to the other side of the car and does the same for her.

Once he's finished with the sisters, he retrieves the kit, folds up the privacy screen, puts both of them in the trunk and closes it. He then climbs into the driver's seat, gathers himself for a moment, and picks up the car's radio mic.

"Dispatch, this is car 49. I've got a code 336, felony pregnancy, two women attempting to cross the state line. … The women have been secured at this time. I will transport to the station at Camp Gerad for processing and disposition. Please send a tow truck to I-35, mile marker 19 to secure their vehicle and tow it to the impound lot."

A moment later, the dispatcher's voice responds. "Roger car 49. Code 336. Transport underway. … Congratulations officer. The state commends you for your actions. Dispatch out."

As the officer starts the engine and prepares to move out on the highway, he looks at the sisters in his rearview mirror. "Comfortable ladies? Enjoy the ride. It's the last chance for either one of you to do so for a very long time."

In the mirror, Susie's face is a mask of defiance while Sarah's expression is one of shocked disbelief. Neither speaks. As the patrol car pulls out onto the highway, the only thing that breaks the silence is the sound of the officer humming to himself as he settles in for the drive ahead.

The Penitent

In contemplation beneath the summer's sun, the Holy One waited by a well alongside a heavily traveled path. From time to time, folk passed by busily engaged with whatever tasks had brought them out in the day's heat. Some gave bits of food or a spare coin to the one who waited but none paused for more than a moment before continuing on their way. Finally though, a penitent came along the path and, seeing the Holy One, stopped to pay respect and ask a blessing.

Filling a bowl with water from the well, the Holy One knelt and washed one foot of the Penitent. Once finished, the Holy One stood, placed the bowl on the ground and brushed off his plain, homespun clothes.

The Penitent waited for several moments before lifting the other foot and offering it also for washing. The Holy One just stood quietly, doing nothing more. Finally the Penitent sighed and said "Well?" offering the dirty foot yet again.

The Holy One, smiling gently, gazed at the foot for just a moment before regarding the Penitent and responding. "I have shown you how my friend. Now you must do the rest yourself." Then he turned and walked to the shade of a nearby tree, leaving the Penitent, with one foot still raised, to wonder at the meaning.

The Penitent stood there looking from the bowl to the Holy One and back again. Finally the Penitent sighed, as if in exasperation, lowered the dirty foot to the ground and turning, began to walk away.

The Holy One, resting in the coolness of the shade, watched as the Penitent slowly moved along the path,

Grieco

merging with the others passing by to become just another traveler on the well-trod way. Then, there beneath the tree, the Holy One returned to contemplation.

By the path, there in the fullness of the sun, the bowl, and the water within it, remained untouched.

The dark side of the Sun

His sturdy, well kempt clothes marked him as different as he stood there, on the sidewalk, watching those who passed by adorned in their finery. He laughed, soft and short, as he lifted his face to the bright light that shone down all around, except on him. He seemed out of place, and his difference slowly drew a crowd, small to be sure, of folk who stopped, and stared, and asked where this stranger could have come from. The light seemed to grow brighter as they gathered near, and, looking at the naked curiosity on their faces, he laughed again, and told them.

"I come from the dark side of the Sun. Oh, I see you smiling, thinking to yourself, 'There's no such place. The Sun's just as bright on the other side as it is on the one we see.' But it ain't. I know. I've been there. I've lived there my whole life. … There's light there alright, but it's dimmer, muted somehow without all the joy and clarity that you folks see every day, shining bright down upon you like it's blessed you with some special grace.

I come from the other side. The place where folks work hard just to get by. The place where nothing is as it seems and folks struggle just to feel alive, really alive in the moments that they're left to themselves to try and sort things through. Never was no real light on that side of the Sun, leastwise none that we could see. Just shadows of the lives we ought to have, that we thought we'd have, that we needed to have to make us feel worthy, here, inside, when we woke up in the morning and as we closed our eyes when we tucked ourselves in bed.

You folks wouldn't know anything about that, standing there basking in the Sun's light. You just take it for granted. It's natural for you. It's always been that way and

it always will be, at least in your minds. But we folks, …
we know a truth that you don't, that the Sun don't always
shine as bright as folks would like, that it's really cold and
miserable on the dark side, where the Sun don't shine the
same as it does here.

Shoot, when I was young, I took for granted that that dim,
muted light was all there was, that that was the way it was
supposed to be, that it was just natural to have less of it. …
I didn't know no better then, and those that did, well they
did their best to hide the truth from me. I'd catch glimpses
of the light, pure and brilliant as it passed by on some
errand, but I thought that was just some special thing, a
chance occurrence that just didn't happen all that often. But
I was wrong. And as I grew, I came to see that the light
always seemed to shine much brighter elsewhere, that the
Sun just didn't favor us as much as it did others who lived
on the other side.

Go on. You can laugh. It's alright. I don't really mind. You
just don't understand. How could you? You've never
known anything but what you have, the Sun shining clear
and bright with the promise that all your tomorrows will be
just like today, with no doubt that the light will always be
there to ease your way across whatever troubles you might
find before you.

But not me. I've had to find my way through darkened
paths as I worked my way towards that brighter light just
there, always just there beyond my reach. Look around you.
Even now as we stand here underneath that selfsame Sun,
the light on you is brighter, more fulsome in its touch upon
your shoulders… and your feet, than upon me and mine. I
keep telling myself that it need not be so, that the Sun
should shine equally upon all folks no matter where they're
from, that if I just work harder and act right and make

believe it ain't so, that I'll be there with you on the bright side where the Sun shines down and everything is easier just 'cause it's so.

But then I look around and see what I always see, that life's not fair, that some folks are just blessed with more sun, that there's no rhyme or reason for it 'cept that it is what it is.

Ain't no changing that. Ain't no getting around the fact that the Sun just shines brighter here. And though you may smile when I say it, though you may disagree as you bask there in that bright and warm spot where you stand. … There just ain't no changing that I come from the dark side of the Sun."

He stopped then, lifting his face to the light as though he could make its touch linger, as those gathered near lost interest and drifted away. He laughed again, short and bitter, as the light dimmed, fading away until only a remnant remained on the spot where he stood, surrounded by light but encased in shadow.

They danced

Growing up, I always looked forward to our visits to grandad's house. He always seemed a magnificent old man to me, full of stories and adventures to be shared with us younger folks. But even then, I remember times when a wistful, sad look would cross his face only to be banished a moment later by a joke and a smile that made the day seem somehow brighter. It was only later when I was more grown, that I began to connect those looks, those moments, with the picture on the mantle of a grandmother I had never known.

I don't remember exactly when I started going with him to visit her. Maybe it was the year we went for a walk in the woods out by his house. We spent the whole day exploring places he'd wandered through when he was a boy. And for whatever reason, at some point we just up and went. Only spent a little time there that first visit, just enough for me to get introduced. To tell the truth, I thought it was a little strange, him talking to her like she was right there, getting to meet me for the first time. But then I realized, that to him, she was, and this was maybe the only time he felt like he was close enough to talk, even if it was pretty much a one-sided conversation.

It became our private thing, those visits. And once I was out and on my own, we'd go to visit her at least once a year, more if my work and travels brought me close enough that I could stop by and visit with granddad. That's where we were today, under the shade of a grand old oak that stood above where she lay. Granddad stood there, hand on the stone that marked her place, faced etched with a grief still strong and deep even after the years passed since she had left. We stayed there in silence for awhile, each deep within our own thoughts, beneath a dark and solemn sky that threatened rain, well suited to our mood.

But then, that ancient man smiled, just a small one at first, like a glimpse of sun struggling to break through all those clouds. I saw him move his hand upon the stone, soft and gentle, more a caress than a pat, as his smile grew broader. He seemed to stand up straighter, suddenly stronger and more vibrant as though escaping, for just a moment, from the cruel tricks that time plays on all of us. He glanced at me in the way I knew meant that he was about to impart some wisdom or just needed to talk to someone he thought just might understand. His eyes grew distant as he looked at something only he could see. And then, with another soft touch upon the stone, he began to speak.

"We used to dance. Oh, I know that doesn't sound too extraordinary, and perhaps it wasn't. After all, we'd dance every chance we could. We used to meet out back when we were kids. She in her pigtails and me in my denim shirt and way back in the woods in that clearing by the little stream, we used to sit and scheme about all the things we'd do when we grew up. And… then after all the talk, we'd make believe we were older than we were, all grown up and facing the world together. We'd pretend we were at some fancy-dress ball surrounded by big shots and society swells. She'd be wearing a fancy gown covered in doo dads and I'd be all in tux with some fancy bow tie to set it all off. And we'd dance, slow and stately, imagining the music that would be playing at those sorts of things.

We kept at it all through our childhood and into our teens, imagining a world that was better than we knew, determined to make our way regardless of whatever we faced along the way. And we fell in love. Oh, I always loved her. Always knew that she was special and that she was the first one I'd want to see on the way to school and the last one to glimpse as dusk drew near and chores and homework drew me back to home. But as we grew older, we fell in love with the kind of constant yearning that folks dream about or maybe read in one of those fancy romance novels.

It didn't matter none that we didn't have two sticks to rub together. We loved each other just the same. And those dances grew longer and more meaningful until we knew, just knew that there was never going to be nobody but each other for the likes of us.

We married. Never mind what folks said about us being too young and foolish to know what was right for us. We knew. And day after day, night after night, we built a life that we could be proud of, that we'd wanted ever since we were little, talking and dancing off in the woods. The babies that followed only made life more complete, more satisfying than we had ever imagined.

'Course it wasn't simple. Nothing ever is. But with each passing year, we managed to carve out a living that was worthwhile. Something that we and our kids could look back on with a knowledge that each and every day was filled with love and happiness.

We still danced, almost every night, only now it was on the hardwood floor in the kitchen of the house we built. We didn't need no music, we heard it loud and clear in our heads just like we'd done all those years ago. The kids would laugh sometimes at us moving in the silent room, but we never paid them no mind, and after awhile they would just sit and watch and even join in until the music in our heads faded away and the dance would come to an end.

Little Book of Stories

Life went on, year after year, with the kids getting older, and eventually moving out on their own. There were heartbreaks and mistakes and all the things that happen to most kids as they grow. But even when they thought things were at their worst, they'd still call or visit and sooner or later they'd reminisce about how we'd dance despite the troubles outside the door and the trials in the world without. It gave them peace to know that that small thing never changed amidst all that did.

And we did dance, even when muscles ached and bones creaked with age, we'd dance, becoming one in each other's arms. It may seem a mystery to some that we should still dance right up to the moment when we couldn't, when one of us would be gone, leaving the other alone for perhaps the first time in our lives. For we knew a love that bore no equal. There was never anyone else. There could never be another. For she was my life and my love, and I was her's and though tomorrow might mark the last day we would ever know together, we would have it no other way. And so, … we danced.

She died, a victim of age and some new disease that appeared out of nowhere to claim her and take her away from me and I miss her more than I can say. Oh, I put on a good face, moving around the empty house, putting up with folks that mean well but really don't have a clue. I mean, she's not really gone. Oh, she is, I do know that. I'm not some old codger living in some dream world. But I've got constant reminders of her at every turn. I expect to see her there, just there, like she always was, waiting with a patient look for me to realize I'd been a fool again, and understand that she'd been right all along about whatever I'd been going on about.

Grieco

I miss her desperately. Still, I've got my memories of our life together, of our talks, our schemes, and the way she'd hold me, tender and true, when the night had come and we were alone with ourselves and our dreams. I see her in the woods at morning, beneath the shaded way at noon, and standing with me at dusk as the stars slowly spark to life in the darkening sky and we danced."

Granddad grew quiet then, hand resting on her stone, still with her dancing under the stars. He stood there for a minute or two recollecting himself before he turned to me once more. He smiled again, a slow, sad smile, the kind you give to tell someone everything will be all right when you know nothing will be ever again. We stood there for awhile longer, respectful of the silence and his lost love. Then granddad softly patted her stone and we turned and headed home.

It did rain later in the day, a soft, misty drizzle, so many tears for a life now gone these many years. We stood on a long, covered porch that marked the front of granddad's house and watched it fall. It seemed somehow fitting to me, that slow mournful fall of water that marked the ending of the day. But granddad didn't seem to mind. He just stood there, looking out towards the woods, watching the wet as it coated every inch of ground and bush between the porch and there. After awhile, he began to sway, just a little, as though he was listening to some music that only he could hear.

I know that he was with her, somewhere deep within his mind, wandering through the woods hand in hand 'til they found that clearing by that little stream... and then, they danced.

Consequences

Grieco

The Sun and the Rooster

The Sun slowly peeked above the world's edge, scattering
the morning fog, and shining warmly down upon the land.
But before the sky was full of light, a rooster, perched upon
its favorite rock, crowed a greeting loud and clear,
competing with Sun for ownership of the day.

Sun looked down upon the rooster, laughed at such a bold
display, and spoke.

"Go on old bird, have your way. How vain and foolish you
are to think that you can challenge me for this day. For I am
the Sun! I will be here tomorrow while you shall not. You
shall grow old while I remain young. I will shine to warm
the world when you are gone and forgotten. Then the day
will be mine alone."

Rooster thought on this before offering his response.

"Perhaps you are right. No one, not even you, knows if
tomorrow will come. Perhaps I will depart, and you will
abide. That is the nature of things. But this day will be mine
always. I may not see tomorrow's dawn, but I have seen
this one. If I am not here, then my children or those like me
shall rule the days that are yet to be.

I may leave, but part of me will be in all that follow as they
embrace their day as I, today, embrace mine. So laugh
young Sun, within the sky so clear, for you will never see a
day so empty as when there is none here to greet you."

And Sun did laugh as it made its way across the sky. But as it did, Sun found itself thinking long upon Rooster's words. And, as the world slept at nightfall, Sun unexpectedly found itself eagerly anticipating the dawn and the chance to win the day from the brash and cocksure Rooster who had spoken so.

But try as it might to approach unobserved before the dawn, it was Rooster, standing tall and calling loud and clear, that announced the day. Seeing the brightening light, Rooster again cried out, with confidence and cheer, welcoming Sun as it crept above the world's edge and rose into the sky. Defeated, Sun continued on its way awaiting the challenge of dawns yet to come.

Eons passed, and Sun, with steady pace, traveled across the heavens bringing dawn and day to every region of the world. And as it did, it slowly grew accustomed to the daily greeting by the brash, crowing roosters on the land below. The world moved easily within Sun's light and as Rooster had predicted, there was always he or his children, or his children's children there to announce the coming of the dawn. And as the days moved on beyond counting, the Sun came to see the calls as a comfort and to look on the roosters with friendship and, just perhaps, with love.

But one day, as night drew near, the last of Rooster's brave brood left the world behind, leaving only memory of cock's sure crow to greet the morning when it next appeared. But even memory quickly faded as the night deepened, the day was forgotten, and the world grew silent.

Grieco

So it was that when Sun did next awake, the day was empty with none to call a greeting and embrace the coming dawn. Sun searched in vain to hear the cry that would so cleanly cut the air each morning. But there was none, and the day was finally the Sun's alone.

Only then, as Sun crept above the world's edge, slowly bringing light to the empty land below, did the true meaning of Rooster's words become clear. For what meaning has Sun, with all its light and warmth, if there is none to greet it and mark its journey across the sky? And in that moment, in that instant of clarified loss, the Sun wept.

Expectations

An old man sat on his porch in his rocking chair and watched the occasional cars pass on the road that ran by his front lawn. After awhile, one stopped just down from the house. There was a flurry of activity as maps were pulled out and studied. Then the car slowly backed up, the windows were rolled down, and the people inside asked for his help.

"Excuse us, but we're lost. Could you tell us where Big City is?"

Moving to where the car was, the old man paused for just a second, smiled and said, "You're not lost at all. Big City is just fifty miles ahead straight down this road. Just keep on going and you'll come right to it."

The people in the car thanked him, rolled up the windows and started to drive off. But after just a short distance, they stopped, the windows came down again, and the car slowly backed up once more to where the old man still stood, watching.

"Excuse us, but could you give us some information."

The old man scratched his head and nodded, saying, "Sure, if I can."

"We're just moving to Big City and don't really know anything about the kind of people there. Could you tell us something about them?"

The old man replied, "Well, what sort of people are you expecting?"

Grieco

"Oh we've heard that they're the nicest people in the world. They're caring and kind and will give you the shirt off their backs if you're in need."

The old man nodded and agreed, "That's the sort of folks you'll find there."

The people in the car thanked him, rolled up the windows, and drove off in the direction of Big City.

A little while later, another car drove past. It also stopped, and maps came out and were studied. After a bit, it too backed up, the windows came down and much the same conversation ensued.

"Excuse me, can you help us? We're lost."

"I'll do what I can." said the old man.

"Can you tell us where Big City is?"

Again the old man smiled and said, "You're not lost at all. Big City is just fifty miles ahead straight down this road. Just keep on going and you'll come right to it."

The people in the car thanked him, rolled up the windows, and started to drive off. But, as before, the car stopped, backed up, and the windows came down once more.

"Excuse us again, but we're new here. Can you tell us what kind of people live in Big City?"

The old man answered in the same way, "What sort of people are you expecting?"

"Well, we understand that they're uncaring, selfish people, who'll steal from you as soon as give you the time of day. You can't trust them as far as you can spit."

Little Book of Stories

The old man nodded gravely and replied, "That's the sort of folks you'll find there."

And with that, the people in the car thanked him, rolled up the windows, and drove off in the direction of Big City.

The old man went back to his chair and sat, musing on how often our expectations determine what we find and how often our expectations reflect ourselves. He sat there a long time, watching the day pass. Then, as dusk slowly began to banish light, he got up and went inside.

John

The sun played with shadows through the trees as the old man sat there, moving gently in his rocker on the front porch. I'd dropped by to check on him and maybe chat for a bit but, as far as I could tell, he was just ignoring me as I stood there at the bottom of the steps. I might as well have been just another lawn ornament, roasting in the sun, waiting for some sort of recognition. Without a breeze, the heat was tolerable, barely, and I eyed the shade of that porch with an anticipation that bordered on exasperation.

He finally glanced my way, nodded just a bit, and motioned for me to take a seat in another rocker situated beside a small table. Once I was settled, he poured two tall glasses of iced tea, from a frosted pitcher, and handed me one. I admit, I was tempted just to drink it all down and ask for more. Instead, I rubbed that glass across my forehead, using the cold glass to chase away the lingering heat. Then, after a moment, I took a sip, savoring the sweetness as I leaned more fully back. We sat there for a good long while slowly sipping our drinks and watching the slowly lengthening shadows. Then, as dusk began to drift across the yard, that old man started to speak.

"The Angel of Death stopped by yesterday. No, no, it wasn't like that. He just happened to be in the neighborhood and thought he'd stop by. Friendly fella. Real neighborly.

We sat on the porch and talked a spell about this and that. Offered him a glass of iced tea… you know… the kind with frost licking at the edges of the glass real nice and cold. Kinda like what we've got now. We chatted about this and that, all the sorts of stuff that neighbors talk about when they get together. Strange thing is, it seemed like I'd known him all my life even though I'd never seen him before he showed up out of nowhere.

Turns out he's a sports fan. Talked about the upcoming season and whether he had a favorite team. He said he did. In fact there was one he was real fond of. Couldn't tell me which one of course. If word got out, there might be talk of favoritism if certain injuries occurred during the season. Not that he'd actually do anything like that mind you, but still, you know how folks talk.

We must have sat there for ages just passing the time of day, watching the wind move the leaves of the trees out there in the yard. Couple of times a deer poked its head through the bushes and, after regarding us for awhile, walked right on up to John.

He asked me to call him John. Pretty awkward saying that "Angel of Death" thing after all.

Yes sir, that deer walked right up to John bold as could be and kinda nuzzled at him 'til he reached out and petted it all gentle like. Sure has a way with animals that John.

Birds, dogs, even that woodchuck that lives under the barn came by to visit with him. At times it almost looked as though they were talking, though not in any language I could understand. Still, they seemed to get along right well, even eating out of his hand after I went and got a loaf of bread and some leftover chicken from the kitchen.

Well, we talked about near enough every subject under the sun from physics to the best way to wean a pup as we watched the shadows cross the yard. 'Cept politics and religion. He said he'd had his fill of politicians, can't say that I blame him, and that religion was a personal matter best left between God and the individual. Figured he was probably right about that and we just sort of let that subject drift on by. Well, we had just a wonderful time sitting

Grieco

there, talking and laughing about this or that. That John sure knows how to tell a joke that's for sure.

But finally, right about sunset, he started to look a little restless. You know, the way someone looks when they have someplace to go but don't want to be impolite or ruin a great day by running off before it has a chance to end natural like. ... So I asked him... straight out... if he had business in these parts.

He stiffened... just a little... then relaxed and gave a rueful smile that challenged the sunset for the rest of the day. He said no, but he did have an appointment somewhere else in the near future. I told him he was welcome to stay awhile longer if he could, maybe play some checkers, or chess if he had a mind to...

He smiled again, and said no, he couldn't stay. He had to get going if he was going to be on time. I said it wouldn't matter all that much if he was just a little late... would it?

He got this far away look in his eyes... you know like when your mind is somewhere else waiting for your body to catch up... and then he looked back at me and thanked me for the day. Seems he didn't get much chance to just sit and be neighborly anymore and he really appreciated the chance to talk.

He was a real gentleman about it. I told him it wasn't nothing.

Stayed awhile longer after all. Played three games of checkers. Beat me each time. But I didn't mind. He's real good company. ... Liked having him around.

He finally did leave though, fading into the shadows on the lawn with the fireflies swarming all around to beat the band. Asked before he left if maybe he could stop by again sometime... just to talk... and maybe play some more checkers. I said that'd be fine and he vanished into the twilight.

Nice fella that John."

And then, as though he'd said all he had to say, that old man just stopped talking. He sat there, gently rocking in his chair, looking out into the yard as though expecting someone to appear out of the gathering dusk. I sat there with him for awhile longer, nursing the last few sips of tea, before taking my leave. As I crossed the yard, I couldn't help but glance behind to see him still sitting there, waiting, as night closed in blurring the edges of the porch until it and he began to merge with the growing darkness.

His words, calm and certain, stuck with me as I walked among the fireflies that danced and swirled to guide me to my home. Nothing to fear. Just a nice chat with the Angel of Death.

"Nice fella that John."

Grieco

As long as the music plays

After a long, lonely drive through the empty night, the sad faced man sat in the roadside bar nursing his drink while listening to music from a jukebox that had seen better days. He chatted with the barman as they watched a young woman, sitting, waiting, at a table near the dance floor.

"You say she comes here every night?"

"Yep. For as long as I've worked here."

"Pretty."

"Very."

"Doesn't drink?"

"She just comes here to dance."

"Who's she waiting for?"

"You'll see. He'll be here any minute now."

As if on cue, the door moved silently. A young man, tall and slim, entered as a cool breeze blew in from the night outside. The woman's face lit up with a smile that transformed her from a somewhat plain, midwestern girl to a radiant beauty. And in that moment, it was clear to see that the two at the bar wished that she was there for them and not the one she so eagerly rose to greet.

"Jim! I was worried. I thought you'd never come!"

He kissed her gently and apologized. "The cows broke loose again. It took me two hours to get them all back in the barn. I came as soon as I cleaned up. Didn't want to look a mess for my best girl."

And as he smiled and pulled her close, she replied, "Your best and only girl!"

They laughed together and the men knew that this must be an old joke between them, the sort of thing that couples gain with long familiarity.

"How long can you stay?" she asked.

"As long as the music plays." came his reply and he led her to the center of the floor.

They began to dance, swaying slowly, clasped together like two lovers held too long apart. The music never stopped, one song after another playing softly, adding to the mood. The shifting melodies made the moment perfect as they moved in unison there beneath the muted lights.

Hours passed like minutes as they danced. From time to time, they gazed deep into each other's eyes and laughed at some whispered joke or smiled when a misstep broke the unison for just an instant.

Occasionally the barman refreshed the drink for the sad faced man who sat, content to sip and watch the two upon the floor. He watched, although he had miles yet to go this night before he'd stop to rest in some flea-bitten motel somewhere off the beaten path in the nowhere that comprised his sales territory. He sat transfixed, watching the two, who, oblivious to all else, danced.

Had he ever been that in love? Had he ever danced that way? Had he ever known the sheer joy of holding that certain someone and forgetting all else except for her, moving sweetly in his arms, as the music played and the night passed?

Grieco

He started as if waking from a dream, took one last sip, and reaching for his wallet prepared to pay. The barman placed one hand upon his arm and said, "Wait."

"What?"

"Just wait."

And with that, the barman turned to the couple and said, "Closing time."

She looked up at her partner. "How long can you stay?" came the question once again, this time almost too soft to hear.

He smiled gently at her and said, as he had before, "As long as the music plays."

"Oh please!" she said to the barman, "Just one more song. Please?"

The barman nodded and began to wipe the bar with a cloth from the sink. The sad faced man glanced questioningly.

"Wait. Just wait."

So he did, and watched the couple move across the floor as music played one final time. As the last notes faded, they seemed to cling more tightly until as silence claimed the room, Jim pulled slightly back with a smile that spoke of regret.

"I have to go."

"I know."

"See you tomorrow?"

"I'll be here."

"I love you."

Little Book of Stories

"I love you."

They kissed and clung to each other for an instant more before Jim turned and stepped away. He paused at the door as if to say something more, then smiled, and as he stood there, hand upon the door, just faded from view.

"What!" cried the sad faced man half rising from his stool.

"Shhh! Wait. Just Wait." came the barman's reply.

The woman, suddenly plain again without her smile, nodded and turned towards the bar. Seeing the sad faced man watching, she smiled again.

"That's just like him." she murmured. "Just like him."

With each word she seemed to fade, slowly merging with the dimness of the room until nothing but the air remained.

Shaking his head in amazed surprise, the sad faced man turned to the barman.

"I don't understand."

"Can't say I do either."

"Who are they?"

"I don't know. I only know they come here each evening and dance until the music stops. Then they fade away."

"Ghosts?"

"I suppose."

"Why do they come here?"

"I don't really know. I guess it's love. She waits for him because she loves him. He comes because she's all that matters to him. They dance because it's the only time they have together."

Grieco

The sad faced man thought on this and reflected on the lonely road ahead.

"How much do I owe you?"

"It's on the house."

The sad faced man paused wallet in hand.

"I was your only customer tonight besides those two. You'll go out of business if your real customers don't pay."

The barman laughed softly.

"Put your wallet away. Heck, it's not about the money. I only came here tonight so they could dance. I guess it gives me hope for the world every time I see them. But it is closing time now. Drive safe. Closing time…"

The sad faced man blinked. And in just that time, the bar was gone. In its place, there was only open countryside, the night air, and moonlight on his face. Gravel crunched beneath his feet as he turned to see his car, now parked by a field of newly mowed hay. He moved quickly to get in, started the engine, and stopped, staring at the space where he knew the bar had been but a moment ago.

Shaking his head, he smiled for the first time and murmured, "Son of a gun."

Then he backed onto the highway, shifted into drive, and sped away. But somehow, the night didn't seem quite as empty anymore.

Consequences

Walking along a country lane, I happened to come upon three men sitting in the morning sun. As I drew closer, it became clear that two of the plainly dressed men were blind while the other suffered from some ailment that rendered his legs useless. Sensing my approach, the three shifted in their spots along the road, perhaps expecting me to stop and spend a few moments with them. I intended to walk past but curiosity got the best of me. I paused, not really knowing what to say but, for no good reason, needing to know what had brought them to this spot. We exchanged some small talk about the warmth of the morning and just how fine a day it would become. Then, as though by common agreement, the men spoke one by one of how they had come to be the men they were today.

The first, trim and neat in a plain but serviceable suit, spoke soft and clear, his sightless eyes wandering across the space in front of him. "I must tell you first of the Djinn, a tricky folk, magical but untrustworthy by their very nature. They have the ability to grant you your deepest desires or even just your merest whims with just a thought, the slightest blink in time for you or I. But one must be careful with them as they have a habit of granting one's desires in perverse ways that are not at all what one might have intended."

I nodded, aware in an instant of the uselessness of the gesture. The third man smiled at my discomfort and told the first to continue with his tale. The first man frowned, as though in frustration at being interrupted, then settled once more into his story. "I knew all this, knew that Djinn could not be trusted, knew that they gave only what they wished, in the way they wished." He shook his head ruefully, "And yet, given the chance to talk with one, my desire got the better of me and I asked for just one thing."

Not sure I believed his tale of Djinn and magic, I interrupted him with what to me seemed like an obvious question. "Wait, how did you know it was a Djinn?"

He turned his head in my direction, his blind eyes searching for the source of my voice. He laughed, a low, pleasant sound against the quiet of the day. "Oh they look just like anyone else. But if you ever saw one, you would know. They exude a sense of purpose, of being that attracts your attention and makes you focus on them and nothing else even as you feel an immediate urge to be anywhere else but in their presence. And yet even with that urge, a sense of fear almost, they charm you, putting you at ease with a gesture, a word, and you forget that you should not pause to linger in their presence.

His very presence fascinated me. And so I stopped and spoke with the Djinn. It went well at first. We spoke of this and that, of his travels around the world and all the things he'd seen. I stood, entranced by the wonders he described. Eventually he asked me of my life and I gladly shared with him my joys and all the little things that seemed so important at the time. I had been cursed with poor eyesight since birth and it must have been clear as I spoke of the impact it had on everything.

Conscious of my poor eyesight, I had a habit of adjusting my glasses as I spoke. The Djinn noticed and eventually asked if there was something he could do to help. I was overwhelmed with gratitude, hope, and fear. For I knew the stories told of Djinn and their capricious nature. But in the end, hope overrode all else. I asked him if he could fix my eyes so I wouldn't need glasses. He looked at me with an intense penetrating look, the way Djinn do. After a moment he asked if I was sure that that was what I wanted. Without a thought, I said, 'Yes.' The Djinn replied, 'So be it.' And since that moment, I've been blind." He laughed again without humor. "And I've certainly had no need for glasses."

With that, the first man fell into a deep, profound silence, shaking his head from time to time as if he continued in some inner dialogue. However, as if taking that silence as a cue, the second man began to speak, raising his eyes to gaze sightless upon the day.

"I too met a Djinn. It was springtime and all was right with the world. We sat in a garden surrounded by flowers just beginning to bloom. We talked of many things, all the time enjoying the sweetness of the air and the exquisite sights of Spring in all its glory. Unlike my luckless friend here..." He gently touched the leg of the first man before continuing. "I had perfect vision and each day was full of wonders as I gazed upon a world of beauty and delight. But I still wanted more. I wanted to see what made these things as they were. Somehow, I must have said as much for he asked if I was dissatisfied with what I saw.

I still remember my surprise at the question, for it summed up in one phrase what I had felt for a long, long time. I wanted to see more. I wanted to see what no one else could see. The Djinn paused, looked at me searchingly and asked if I was certain that was what I wanted. Sure of what I meant, I did not hesitate in saying yes. But as the Djinn said, "Then so be it." The sight ebbed from my eyes, leaving me as you see me now."

He sighed deeply, wringing his hands held loosely in his lap. "He gave me what I said I wanted." He raised one hand and tapped the side of his head. "Now no one can see what I do, here within my mind." Finished, he let his hand drop to his lap once more and sat gazing at what only he could see.

Grieco

After a moment, the third man cleared his throat, rousing me from my thoughts. Turning to him, I noted a faint look of what could pass for amusement cross his face. "I imagine that your story is similar to your two friends here?"

The third man smiled, his eyes clear and vibrant as he took in me, the two with him, and the day around him. He paused for just a moment, as if gathering his thoughts and then spoke.

"My story is like theirs in all ways that matter. I too met a Djinn, apparently by chance, while sitting outside by myself at a sidewalk café enjoying a leisurely lunch. Like many others, the Djinn seemed to be just another passerby out enjoying the warmth of the summer's day. Unlike those others, the Djinn paused, then stopped, apparently drawn to the café. After looking around for a place to sit, he asked if I would mind if he shared my table. I felt all the things, my friend there described..." He motioned towards the first man, sitting to his right. "...intense focus, fear, and urge to be away, and a sense of charm and attraction that overrode all else. Despite my better instincts, I invited him to sit."

He paused for a moment, shaking his head as if still amazed that he would have done such a thing, and then continued. "And ultimately, I was glad I did. The Djinn was charming, the perfect lunch companion. We talked for over an hour sharing jokes and stories of our lives. But eventually the meal was done, the bill came, and the time came for us to go our separate ways. As he prepared to leave, the Djinn thanked me for letting him share my table and casually asked if there was anything he could do for me.

Now, unlike my friends here," he nodded to his two companions, "I was content with what and who I was. I wanted for nothing that I considered important. I had friends. I had enough money to do what I wanted when I wanted. I considered myself lucky to have the freedom to follow my own course in life. So, after thinking for a minute or two, I told him no. I was fine, and I thanked him for his company. He turned to go and at the last, just as I thought he would leave, he turned back one more time and asked, 'Are you sure there's nothing?'

Frankly, he caught me off guard. I had already moved on in my mind to the rest of my day and all the little things I would do to fill it. I didn't really have an answer. I truly didn't intend to answer him. But for some reason I still don't completely understand, I said I just didn't understand why some folks did the things they did, why they didn't appreciate what they had and looked for things they didn't need. I guess, I said that I would like to better understand the consequences of human desire.

As soon as I spoke the words, I knew, knew that somehow, in some fashion the Djinn would make me pay for my errant words. But he just smiled, and I felt perhaps it would be ok after all. Then he softly said, 'So be it.'"

He stopped speaking then, seemingly at a loss for how to continue. After a moment, I broke the silence that stretched between us. "And that is when you lost the use of your legs?"

He glanced up at me, laughing with a joy that somehow made the day seem brighter. "Ah no, no my friend. I was born this way." He gestured at his useless legs. "I had made my peace with my condition long before I met the Djinn." He paused for a second and then gestured at his two companions. "It was then that he put me with these two."

He laughed again and changed the subject to other things. I enjoyed his candor and his view of things and, despite myself, lingered in conversation. But eventually, mindful of the time and tasks that awaited my attention, I took my leave and continued down the lane to what yet lay ahead.

Grieco

All was well. Birdsong filled the air. The sun shone brightly in the clear blue sky and the country lane was peaceful and serene. It was all anyone could possibly want and more. But even as I strolled, I could not help but think of those three strangers and the consequences of human desire.

Hell or high water

She hadn't expected to be here, not in this thrift shop in the run-down old brick warehouse where the mill used to store its products. Not that she'd never been here before. She used to drop in from time to time, dropping off old clothes or a piece of furniture that the family had outgrown. But she'd never had to shop here, never had to look for bargains, sorting through what other folks had discarded.

There'd been no reason for her to even think of thrift shops before. Her husband's job at the mill had been secure, a safe job that guaranteed they'd have enough to pay off the mortgage, raise a family, and maybe splurge a bit now and then. They'd never really had to wonder how to make ends meet as long as they were fairly prudent in how they spent his pay.

Of course, that was before the accident at the mill, an explosion caused by a spark that ignited the dust and accompanying gas that was a byproduct of the manufacturing process. Her husband had been one of the lucky ones, working at the other end of the mill when it happened. He'd gotten out with just a few cuts and bruises and had worked for the next forty-eight hours straight trying to get to those who hadn't made it out.

They'd rescued some, found others, and then the town had gone into a sort of collective mourning period, shocked that anything like this could've happened here, full of sorrow for the hurt and dead, and worried about what the future would bring.

The company did what they could, what they ought to have done. They commiserated with the town, gave condolences to the families of the dead, gave insurance and disability payouts to those who were hurt. They even gave their word that they would rebuild, that the mill would be better than before, upgraded with all the latest technology, that all the jobs would be safe. It would take a little time to rebuild, but it would happen.

'Course it never did. Folks waited, healed their hurts as best they could, and trusted that the company would keep its word. It came as a surprise when the news broke that the company had opened a new mill elsewhere, a real shock to those that had trusted the company to do the right thing. The news was a crippling blow to families that had counted on the mill reopening. Her husband's job disappeared with all the rest, and they'd had to scrimp and cut corners ever since.

Oh they got by, somehow. Her husband managed to scrape together an income from day work and odd jobs he found. She did her part as best she could, finding new ways to reuse older items, passing hand-me downs from one kid to another, picking up essentials at garage sales, and stretching things beyond their use.

Which brought her to today and the reason she was looking through what she might have once thought of as junk. Brand Spanking Used the thrift store sign read. She thought that might be a bit too kind for most of this stuff. So she fought to contain a surge of hope when she caught sight of a beat-up wooden dining table off by itself against the far wall.

The table bore the marks of time with its share of scratches and dents and even a few discolored spots where hot pots had been placed on its wooden surface. Yes, it was clearly used, but it was a damn sight better than the old folding card table they had been using until today. This table, despite its age and its flaws, was oak, or at least it looked like it, although it could have been some clever veneer that made it look that way.

Little Book of Stories

It didn't really matter. It was big. Big enough to fit her entire family at one seating without anyone having to pretend to like the "game" of camping on a set of mismatched, oversized pillows discovered at the thrift store sometime last year.

It was solid. Solid enough to withstand the demands of a growing family and children that all too often pushed when they should have pulled and whose roughhousing was responsible for her being here now. The kids, God bless them, had been running and wrestling, like kids do, when they'd smashed right into that worn out card table. Broke one of the legs clean off. No way to fix it. Nothing to do but to leave it where it lay on the linoleum and come out to find something to replace it.

Frankly, she was surprised she had found anything at all in her price range, especially something like this table. Oh, she was thankful, over the moon happy she had found it. But she couldn't imagine why anyone would have gotten rid of this. Certainly not at this price. It was cheap. Cheap enough that even she could afford it on her limited budget. Without a second thought, she flagged down the first store worker she could find and started gently haggling to try and get the delivery thrown in for free. No matter if she couldn't. She would get this table come Hell or high water. A few bucks more for delivery would be a price she was more than willing to pay… if she had to.

<>

His full zip hoody with large black, white, and red checkered squares made him stand out as he stood there at the entrance of the alley. He was motionless, waiting for something or someone in the cold morning air. He faced away from the street as though afraid that someone, in a passing car or perhaps just walking by, might recognize him and stop to talk or lend a helping hand. He looked better off than he was, hoody and jeans seemingly clean and still relatively new.

He knew he ought to consider himself lucky. He'd had a good job at the mill. Been given the house by his parents when they'd moved to Florida a few years back. No real bills to speak of. Even thought of settling down at some point once he'd found the right person to spend his life with. But that had all changed in a flash when the mill had gone up.

It was just another day, a crisp clear one if he remembered right. He was working down on the floor towards the center of the mill when it happened. Folks all around were joking and laughing at some prank one of them had pulled. A harmless thing really, the sort of things guys do to one another to relieve the boredom and tedium of the job. One moment everything was fine. The next, everything was chaos with bricks and steel and beams and equipment and people flying every which way at once. Yeah, he'd been lucky. Even though he'd been trapped under debris with his right leg crushed, there were a lot of his friends who'd been killed right there and then.

He had been trapped for what seemed like an eternity, in pain so intense he might have blacked out a few times. All he could really remember of that time was a surreal stillness as a thick haze of dust and pulverized brick slowly drifted down all around. And the agony... oh yes, the agony rolling through him to the extent that he'd wished that the debris shifting above him would finally fall and end it all.

It had been hours, though it seemed much longer, when rescuers had finally found him. It took longer still for them to stabilize the broken metal and bricks that had trapped him. They managed to cut him free but not before an EMT had given him a shot of something that had numbed the searing pain to a dull background presence and allowed him to observe, in some small part of his mind, what was going on around him.

They'd rushed him to the hospital where he went through hours of surgery. The docs had tried desperately to fix his leg, but it was pretty much a lost cause. Still they'd done miracles. Actually had saved it, although it would never be what it had been before. The bones had been crushed in too many places for that and steel rods and pins would never replace what nature had provided in the first place.

They'd put him on permanent disability and given him pills to manage the pain. Didn't hesitate to give him refills for the first year as the pain slowly subsided to an inconvenience, then to a faint background, and finally to just an occasional nuisance when he tried to do something beyond the limited ability of his reconstructed leg. But when the docs had decided he was fine, or as fine as he'd ever be, they'd stopped giving him refills, more or less forcing him to go cold turkey.

He'd tried, really he had, but he just wasn't strong enough. His need for the pills remained, even as the pain ended, and seemed to grow stronger even as he tried to wean himself off them. But he was lucky there as well. He had his company and state disability to fall back on. It wasn't much, but it was enough to get by most months with just enough left over to somehow find some meds from the gray market that had sprung up in the town as folks had slowly lost hope that the mill was ever coming back.

Still, it had been getting harder and harder to find what he needed, and he had had to slowly start selling some of his things to meet his needs as street prices had climbed to match the shortage. He was almost forced to move to cheaper "alternatives", but he'd been lucky again when another survivor from the mill had cued him in on a new supply. Turned out to be one of their former co-workers… good guy… you could trust him… who had secured a steady stock of pills.

Oh, there still were occasional shortages and that meant the price would be steeper on some months. But at least he had his pills, even if he did still sometimes have to sell some stuff to make ends meet. He felt bad about it, especially when it was something that had sentimental value. But he had no choice. It was either that or…

So there he was, hand clenched around the hundred dollars in his left pocket. He hadn't wanted to sell the table, but there had been no other choice. He'd needed the money and that table was the only thing left guaranteed to get it quickly.

The man at the thrift shop had shaken his head, seemingly hesitant to buy another item from him but he hadn't turned him away either. Eventually, after a show of examining the table and pointing out its flaws, the man had offered a price far too low for its value, knowing from past experience that any offer would be quickly accepted.

And it had been. Reluctant as he might have been in another life to let the table go, here and now in this life, in this god-awful checkered hoody, he'd had no choice. It had been his family's table, new when they had gotten it so many years before. He had spent his youth and teenage years around it and he still carried memories with him of meals and game nights shared with family and friends.

But that was long ago, at least if his mind could be trusted. His mind wasn't as clear as it had been then, back before the accident, back before the docs had given him meds to control the pain and then denied him more once they said he was healed. But it was tightly focused on the here and now and his urgent need for what he waited for, there at the alley, in the cold December sunshine. The price wouldn't be cheap, it never was, but he would pay what was asked for, come Hell or high water, to get what he needed. And so he waited, hands softly shaking, with his growing need more urgent as the minutes passed.

<>

He sat in the diner and watched the man in the checkered hoody as he stood there motionless across the street. He slowly picked at his ham and eggs, remnants of some pancakes resting on a plate to his right. He had time yet. The man across the street could wait awhile more. There was no pacing, no head movement that would come as the demand increased and the urgent search for relief became more obvious to one who knew what to watch for. There was still time to finish and maybe even have a second cup of coffee before going to his appointment. After all, the hoody wasn't going to go anywhere.

Lingering over his morning meal, the man in the diner reflected that he hadn't always been this way, hadn't always been so casual about profiting from other folks' misfortune. He used to help out folks like that guy across the street, used to think poorly of people taking advantage where they should have been supportive. But that was before the explosion at the mill and he'd found himself in the soup line along with all his coworkers and their families.

Oh, he'd found day work and odd jobs here and there, still did if truth be told, but it was never enough to replace the income he'd lost. Made it hard to support a growing family. Meals around that old card table had become more and more strained as savings shrank and he and his wife stared into a future that held little promise for them or their kids.

Grieco

He was always looking for an edge up. For something that would ease the burden, if just for a little while. He'd ask around, spreading the word that he was handy, available for work, and flexible as to whatever hours were required. Probably wasn't surprising then when a buddy gave him a tip on a prospective job. Easy money. Kind of a delivery service that needed part time folks. Possibility for advancement if you did well. Could still do other stuff as well.

Sounded good. Maybe too good, but he couldn't afford to be too choosey. He'd gone to the meet, watched as his buddy vouched for him, and listened as the stranger in the six-hundred-dollar suit had made his pitch. Pharmaceutical delivery servicing an under-supported population. Helping bring relief to folks who had fallen through the system. Bringing needed meds across the last mile of the supply train. It all sounded good. Heck, it seemed good at first, seeing those looks of relief as he delivered pills and other items to the folks on his route, taking their cash in return.

He got to keep a percentage of the take, relatively small at first but then increasing as he got more referrals and his deliveries began to grow in volume. It was inevitable that he'd slowly come to see things for what they were, that his deliveries were just drug drops for an agreed price to folks who had exhausted other options. He thought about stopping. Yeah, he thought long and hard, but the money was too good. Not great mind you. Most of it went to the Suit but what he kept made a difference at home, smoothing out the rough spots until he could find something better. It took him awhile to realize that there wasn't anything out there. This was as good as it was going to get, and he'd better just make the best of it.

It was an accident really the first time he charged one of his customers more than the asking price. There'd been a delay in getting the product to town and the woman had been too long without. She was desperate. Willing to do anything, pay anything to get her pills. When she'd pushed twice the asking price into his hands, he just accepted it, but he'd understood the possibilities immediately. Only turned in the normal amount. When nothing happened, he started experimenting. He'd be a little late with deliveries. Hike up the anxiety levels of individual customers. Noticed pretty quick, that if he timed the delivery right, he could increase the price and they wouldn't blink an eye. All he had to do was put it down to a periodic supply shortage. They might grumble a little, but they'd still buy. What other choice did they have?

Still in all, he knew that if he did this all the time, he might lose folks to cheaper alternatives, his route would suffer, and word would eventually get back to the Suit. So he never hit the same customer twice in a row. He spaced it out, rotating between folks so the burden wouldn't be too much, and they'd continue of think of him as a friend providing a service instead of a crook extorting them for as much as he could.

Today it was checkered hoody's turn. Oh he had a name. They all had names, but he preferred not to think of them that way. Some of them had even been friends, or at least co-workers at the mill, back before the accident. They'd worked together, played together, even watched each other's kids from time to time. Kind of one big family looking out for one another.

No, he didn't use their names. Didn't even think of them that way anymore. It made it easier to do this. And he had to do this to make ends meet, to put food on the table, and handle those unexpected things that cropped up. Like today... the kids had broken that old card table at home, and he'd promised the wife she could get a new table.

Grieco

Something mcre durable, wooden maybe that could survive what the kids could dish out. He'd go through Hell and high water before he'd disappoint that little lady. Some extra cash today would mean he wouldn't have to.

He glanced out the window again. Almost time. Checkered hoody guy had begun to fidget, shifting slowly from foot to foot and then starting to slowly pace back and forth in the mouth of the alley. Yeah, ready. He passed on the coffee refill, paid his check, put on his winter jacket to ward off the chill, and walked across the street.

Think of Socrates

Two friends sat upon a park bench beneath an azure sky. A canopy of trees shaded them from the brilliant sun as birds sang and flew among the branches. A perfect day for sitting, a perfect day for talking, as friends do when alone.

"Power. Ah, to have the power of a King. To rule billions of people and to enforce your will upon the multitudes. Now that's power."

"That's not power."

"Ah but it is. To hold the world in one's hand and to be able to crush what displeases one or build upon what one deems worthy. That is power."

"Why?"

"With such authority and power one can shape the future. One can make the world as it should be. One can help the needy, feed the hungry, right wrongs, and halt injustice."

"Laudable, but wrong."

"What do you mean, wrong? These are all things any right-minded person would do if they had the opportunity. Eliminate the problems that exist. Help those that need it most."

"Those are all things that you would do. But everyone does not share your view. What if such "power" were given to one who thought otherwise? Who believed that all is as it should be? That the few who are blessed with riches and comfort and goods and health were so because they were predestined to have them, and that those who did not were doomed to their existence in much the same way? What happens then?"

Grieco

"Your point is well taken. But there have always been those who tried to put themselves above others regardless of the cost incurred. They may have their day, but, in time, they are replaced and forgotten as others who care more deeply for humanity arise."

"Exactly."

"Exactly?"

"They are replaced. They fall. They lose their "power" and all they tried to do is replaced by the new work of those now in control."

"Yes. The good replaces the bad."

"And humanity is the better for it?"

"Yes."

"Then that must hold true as well for those with more altruistic motives."

"What?"

"The good must eventually relinquish or lose "power"."

"So?"

"And the bad will replace the good in some instances."

"I suppose that's possible."

"And the good that has been done will be replaced by the work of those now in control…?"

"What is your point!"

"Think of Socrates."

"Socrates?"

Little Book of Stories

"Who now remembers the names of those who signed his death warrant? Yet we remember him and his philosophy."

"What has that got to do with what we are talking about?"

"Everything."

"I don't understand."

"What are we talking about?"

"Power."

"Yes, and the ability to shape the world as we believe it should be."

"What has that got to do with Socrates? He was an ancient Greek with no importance to today's world."

"Yet we study him in our schools. We are immersed in his philosophy of life and state and existence related to us by his student Plato."

"So?"

"Those thoughts, along with the thoughts of other philosophers and poets and story tellers have shaped who we are and what we believe about the right of things."

"But they did nothing in their times. They neither built nor ruled nor held sway during times of crisis, during victory and defeat. They had no "power"."

"Buildings fall. Rulers die. Crises come and go. Yet the thoughts of these few remain. Who knows now the name of the rulers of Athens? Yet most remember Socrates. Who now knows the ministers of governments long forgot? Yet most have heard of Shakespeare, or Keats, or Burns, or Frost, or Plato. And if we know not their names, then still their thoughts resound in books and plays, and a thousand other things because they have influenced the way we think, the way we live, the things we believe."

"But thoughts will not feed the hungry."

"True. But they may shape your belief that one should feed the hungry."

"Ah…".

"Indeed. Ah, to be a poet and philosopher. To shape the future with words and thoughts. To touch the minds of generations yet unborn and shape their worlds with truth and feelings from a place long vanished in the mists of time. Now that, that, is power."

No choice

She'd had no choice.

And that's why she was here, in the backroom of a rundown building in the middle of someplace. Someplace she had never thought she would be. Someplace she wouldn't have had to be, back when she'd had a choice, back when the world was simpler, back before she'd been violated, her innocence stolen, and her illusions of the world shattered.

She had tried other routes. She attempted to tell her mother, but she wouldn't listen, didn't want to hear, didn't want to know what her husband had done, was continuing to do right up to last night when he came home, stinking of drink, and climbed the stairs to where his daughter lay dreading his footfalls on the old wooden steps and the creaking of the floorboards as he entered her room.

She tried to tell the church, but they blamed her, saying it was a sin to have sex out of wedlock, not believing that such a God-fearing man like her father could have done such a thing, and demanding the name of the boy she was so obviously protecting with her lies.

She went to the police, but they needed some kind of proof, some adult to verify her story, to show that she wasn't just some hysterical girl trying to get back at her father for some imagined slight or some punishment he had rightfully meted out. And besides, who'd take the word of a kid who didn't have sense enough not to get knocked-up in the first place?

She even tried to tell her friends, but the ones she told shunned her and whispered behind her back until she could feel the eyes of the entire school watching her, judging her, shaming her with their awkward silence and every glance that quickly turned away as she passed by.

And so, at fifteen, she'd had no choice; raped by her father, pushed away by her mother, blamed by her church, disbelieved by the police, shunned and shamed by her friends. When a former classmate had told her that she knew someone who could help, could end this constant torment, and give her back her life, she listened. And when she could stand no more, when it all became too much to bear, when her soul ached with every breath and the only hope she had was to end her life or do this, she acted.

She scrimped and saved her allowance and worked odd jobs to raise the money she would need. Cash, it could only be cash, so there would be nothing to trace, no trail for vigilantes or bounty hunters to follow once it was done.

She had hesitated, but only for a second, outside the door to this place, uncertain, despite the assurances of her former classmate, that this was safe, that this was the only answer other than that… more permanent solution. But once that door was opened and then closed behind her, it had all gone quickly, perhaps too quickly, as cash changed hands and she'd been scraped clean while lying on an unpadded table slowly bleeding into a wad of towels placed to catch the blood and detritus from the procedure.

The bleeding was normal, she was told, and would soon stop. It hadn't, and the frightened look on the masked face told her more than she wanted to know. The sound of the closing door was her first clue that she'd been abandoned to die there on that table, in the backroom of a rundown building in the middle of someplace. She knew it as she weakened, her lifeblood flowing from her body into the waiting towels and, from them, onto the floor. And as the light faded from her eyes, taking with it all that she was and all she might have become, she thought "Damn them. Damn them all to Hell." and was gone.

She'd had no choice.

Djinn

I was sitting in the booth of a fast-food joint, burger in
hand, milkshake before me, and a sweet, twenty-three-year-
old redhead next to me hanging on my every word, or
pretending to. Sometimes it's just hard to tell.

"You sure you want to hear this?"

She turned towards me, swiveling in her seat until she was
facing me, soft brown eyes probing mine for something
only she might see.

"Yes. Yes, I do."

She casually sipped from her cola and munched on a couple
of fries she'd picked up from the tray in front of her before
continuing.

"I'm fascinated by the stories people tell. They're never
quite what I expect but they're always very revealing about
the person and the life they've led."

She paused for a second, considering me with a measuring
look I'd seen before on the faces of women who thought
that I just might be "the one".

I smiled and shook my head at what that look implied.
"Well, I'm sure that my story is a little stranger than most."

"Oh I don't know." she said, her mouth curving upward
into a smile that told me she knew what I was thinking.
"I've heard some pretty strange stories."

"Not like this."

Little Book of Stories

"Why don't you let me be the judge of that."

I paused, staring at my hands, thinking hard about how to begin. "Well if you're sure."

"Yes. Come on. Tell me." She settled into a listening pose, chin on her hands and waited expectantly for me to begin.

"Well ok then. Let me see. … It was a Monday. I had come into the city to pick up some things I needed for a job I was working on. I suppose I could've gotten them closer to home, but I wanted the best I could get and besides, it gave me an excuse to get away for a day. Kill two birds with one stone. Get those things and kind of have a day off at the same time."

I looked at her for a moment for some sign that she really was interested. She smiled again and nodded for me to go on.

"I had stopped to tie my shoe when I saw him. No one else seemed to. A nondescript man in simple clothes, he had just stopped a child from falling as she skated among the folks upon the crowded sidewalk. Yet no one seemed to notice, least of all the girl, as all continued on upon their way.

I stared. I confess I could not help myself, completely forgetting why I had stopped. Perhaps it was because of that and my continued stillness in a sea of motion that led him to notice me. He paused, a small frown appearing as, with pursed lips, he contemplated me. Then, tugging at his clothes as though to smooth some imagined flaw, he made his way to me.

Grieco

As he moved, I stared with open mouth as people stepped round him with never a glance at whom they passed. Soon, too soon it seemed, he stood before me, a place of calm upon the concrete way. Examining me closely, a smile slowly spread upon his ageless face as he leaned nearer and said, "Do you see me?"

My eyes grew wide in shocked surprise and I sought words to stammer forth a weak reply, "Y – Y – Yes. Why, should I not?"

He laughed, a pleasant sound, and smiled again.

"Most do not. But it does occur occasionally." Bending to tie my shoe, he continued, "These waxed laces tend to slip, you must double knot them if you wish to have them grip and stay throughout the day."

Dumbfounded, I remained still as he tied them as a parent would do for a child. As he straightened up I found my voice again and asked,

"Who are you?"

He thought for an instant before he replied as though the words would in some way affect the movement of the world around us.

"A man," he said, "like you in many ways. Yes, a man with a talent, more a gift, that is unshared by any."

He turned as if to go and I reached to grab his jacket for there was more I wanted to know.

"Who, who are you? And how do you move unnoticed here among the crowd?"

Little Book of Stories

He turned back and paused, his eyes meeting mine to see my confused need to know what was happening.

With a wave of his hand everything went still, and silence lay thick upon us. Bewildered and surprised, I asked, "What have you done?"

He smiled again, a welcome sight, and somehow reassuring in spite of the strangeness of our meeting.

"Ah, that is a different question, but I will answer it first since it is more easily said. I have placed us between instants, in the place that occupies the space between the ticking of the clock, in a sense, between seconds, as the world knows them. Time moves differently here. A thousand years would pass within this space and still no eyelid would have blinked upon that passing girl."

"You do not mean to leave me here..."

"No! No... It is merely more convenient to use this place to answer your questions."

"But, But ... "

With a gesture he bid me wait and leaning back against a lamppost began to speak.

"Who am I? Perhaps it is easiest to say that I was once as you are now. Then I saw the one who walked between the rain, and everything changed on that day."

"The one who walked between the rain?"

He paused and laughed gently at my obvious confusion.

Grieco

"Oh yes, he walked between the rain. Maybe it would help if I started at the beginning.

It was long ago, and I was young, about the age you are now. My village was near the shore of the Inland Sea, and we were poorer than the ground we farmed.

It had rained for what seemed like months, although in truth it had been but three days. Still, I was miserable, filthy, and wet to my core. The ground was one massive mix of mud and water where one could get wet or covered with slop depending on the chance misstep or moment's inattention. I had had both in full measure that day and was disgusted with my lot in life.

It was then, in the midst of my misery that I saw him. At first, I thought my mind was playing tricks on me, that I was seeing phantoms. For there, not twenty feet away, as I picked myself up from yet another visit to the muck beneath my feet, was a man, perfectly dry, appearing to dance beneath the rain. Yet, despite the constant downpour, he remained untouched by it. I was so surprised I sat back down into the mud and stared openmouthed as he continued to dance untouched beneath the rain.

Time lost all meaning to me as I sat and watched in open disbelief. But, as I watched, I saw that he was not dancing. Rather, he was weaving in and out between the raindrops as they fell, smiling all the time as though it was a kind of game whose rules were known to him and him alone. I must have laughed, convinced I was mad or at best in the presence of a god who would presently notice me and squash me like a bug and leave me here to sink beneath the surface of this muddy ground with no trace I had ever existed, never to be found.

Little Book of Stories

He turned then and, as if seeing me for the first time, paused, then stopped his game to examine me as one might examine the first flower at the birth of Spring. He came closer, still untouched by rain that drenched me as he drew near, And then he said a most amazing thing.

"Do you see me?"

Being faced with a god is no small thing, but being spoken to by one is more than I could bear under the circumstances. Throwing myself as best I could face down within the muck I cried, "Yes my Lord, I see thee. Do not destroy your humble servant but spare me that I may spread the news of your arrival."

Bemused, he regarded me a moment and said, "Well, I guess that answers that."

Reaching out to grab me by the arm he continued, "Come, come man. Stand up. Get out of the mud. Here, let me help you."

And with that he lifted me as easily as a child would a toy and set me on my feet. I cowered, hiding my face, for one must not look upon a God until given permission.

Considering me with dark, deep-set eyes, he spoke again. "What exactly do you think I am?"

"A god!" I replied, "Although which one I confess I do not know. Forgive me my ignorance. I do not mean to offend…"

He laughed, and the sound of it caused me to peer from out my hands to see if I had pleased him with my response.

Grieco

"A god. I like the sound of that." He laughed again, deep and rich in tone, and reaching out, moved my hands away from my face.

"Come man, look at me."

I did, to be rewarded with a smile. Regarding me he said, "We must do something about that mud." and with a wave of his hand I was clean, and dry, and standing on a patch of firm ground now untouched by the rain still falling all around just beyond my reach.

"There that's better."

"You ARE a god!" I said, examining myself and marveling at my now clean clothes.

"I suppose you might think so." came the reply, "But I am not."

I could not restrain myself. "But if you are not a god... then what are you?"

Smiling yet again, he scratched his head and thought for a moment.

"I suppose you could call me a Djinn. Yes. That would be closest to the truth."

A Djinn! Every child knew the stories of these mighty spirits who could move mountains with the barest thought or could level a city with the merest flick of a finger. They were huge monstrous demons only held in check by limits placed upon them in the ancient past by the wisest of men. Now they could only work their evil by granting the wishes of men and twisting the result to suit their ends. A Djinn!

Little Book of Stories

"You do not look like a Djinn." I said cautiously, trying not to offend.

"What? Oh… the stories." He sat on a stool where there had been none an instant before. "Those stories aren't true. We're not monsters you know."

"But you have power. The rain, my clothes, the stool… "

Nodding, he continued, "Of course, of course. Yes, we have power, great power to change things as we see fit. But we do have… limitations."

"But what of the wishes?"

"The wishes?" He looked blankly at me for an instant before understanding slowly spread across his face.

"Oh you mean the wishes by which the Djinn work their way through men like you?"

I nodded, now caught up in the chance I thought presented to me.

"Since you are here and have already done much for me, do you intend to offer me the wishes?"

Clearly amused, he laughed so hard his face turned red. Finally he caught his breath and turned to where I stood still as a deer awaiting a lion's charge.

"I suppose if it did no harm, I could grant you one wish. What is it you desire?"

I could not believe it! I, a peasant from the meanest farm in the poorest village in the most infertile part of all the land, was to be given a wish by a Djinn. I had dreamed of this from the time I was a child and first heard the stories. Over the years, I had thought hard of how to avoid the traps set by the Djinn for the unwary until I had come to only one possible wish that would give me what I wanted without reliance on the good faith of the monster Djinn. With that in mind, I paused to make certain the words would be correct and in the order meant. I would get only one chance!

"I wish that I had all your powers and abilities without any of the limitations placed upon you." I declared in as firm a voice as I could muster and looked the Djinn squarely in the eyes.

I could tell he was startled by the wish and the smile left his face as though a cloud had passed in front of the sun.

"You do not know what you ask."

"I do!" I cried, "And you are bound to grant me this by the ancient laws set upon you."

He stared at me for a moment and then shook his head. "The stories again… Still, it will do no lasting harm… and you did see me… perhaps…"

His gaze took on a faraway look and I began to fear that I had overreached myself when, at last, he shook himself.

"Very well. Your wish is granted."

"That's it!" I said. "That's all there is to it?"

He smiled ruefully, "Were you expecting thunder and lightning and a puff of smoke perhaps?"

Little Book of Stories

"Well yes, or something more than just, your wish is granted. I don't feel any different."

He smiled again, but it seemed more sadly now, "You will. You will. It will come upon you slowly but before long you will have all that you wished for."

"Am I a now a Djinn?"

"You did not wish for that. No, you are not a Djinn, but you are now no longer a man either. You are perhaps a little of both. I hope you do not come to regret your wish."

"I will not." I said, certain that everything I ever wanted would now be mine.

"Perhaps." he replied. "Well, what is done is done. Tell me of yourself and your life here."

Completely forgetting the fear I'd felt earlier, we talked for what seemed like hours, him asking questions and I talking of the world I knew. I learned little of him or where he came from and all too soon he stood, stool vanishing behind him.

"Well, I guess it's time for me to go." he said and turned as if to leave.

"Wait!" I cried. "You have not told me how to use the powers you have given me!"

"You did not wish for that did you?" came the words, and I cringed thinking I had been trapped despite my careful phrasing of the wish.

Grieco

As he turned to leave he spoke, throwing the words over his shoulder as he moved away.

"Oh it will come to you. You will simply know that you can. Knowledge helps. The more you know the more you can do. But it's a matter of will my boy. If you will something, it will simply be. You'll see. You'll see."

And with that, he moved off into the rain again, weaving and moving in between the drops until he disappeared from view. I stood inside the dry space for yet a while and stared at the rain falling just an arm's length away. I *felt* no different. My hands were still my hands, my arms my arms, my feet… well you get the idea. I moved a little to one side and reached my hand toward the rain. When it passed whatever hidden boundary the Djinn had left, I felt the rain, cold and wet, splashing off my fingers. I quickly drew it back, looking at the water on my hand in disbelief.

"It didn't work." I muttered. I tried it several times more with the same results, each time muttering more loudly than the last.

Suddenly, without warning, the bubble of no rain vanished as if it had never been. I was drenched as a deluge of rain poured down upon me, soaking me through in a matter of seconds. "NO!" I yelled. "IT ISN'T FAIR. I WANT TO BE WARM AND DRY!" and I was. The rain still hit me. I could feel it. But it did not penetrate my clothes. They were once again as dry as before. It was as if an invisible barrier had been placed which stopped the water from getting into the material. It just rolled off. And my hair and skin remained dry even though I could see the raindrops bouncing off my hand.

Little Book of Stories

I stood there transfixed and stared at my hand for a long time, moving it this way and that, watching the rain hit and fall away leaving it dry. I laughed and laughed as the realization of what had just occurred came to me. I was a Djinn! Or if not a Djinn, then a man with the powers of one!

I stood there a long time practicing until I was comfortable with my new power. I made a small bubble around me where the rain could not go, and let the ground be dry where I would walk. I even conjured up a bowl of porridge when I realized I was hungry. It was good, not like my mother's mind you, but good all the same and filled my present need for food. Finally, convinced I had things well in hand, I turned and set off back to my village.

It was a pleasant walk without the mud and muck to slow me down and soon I was on the hill above the place where I was born. It looked no different. The twelve small thatch houses, huts really, stood within the low stockade, awash in water and mud. Animals huddled miserably against the building walls, trying unsuccessfully to get out of the rain. My mother struggled as she tried to walk across the enclosure, a wooden pail in hand half-filled with scraps from the mid-day meal. Geese, squawking loudly, gathered round her to get first grab at whatever morsels she would soon empty on the ground.

I remember thinking of how hard she had always worked and how that would no longer be necessary now that I possessed the power of the Djinn. How wet and cold she looked as she tended there to the animals. This would never do. Still uncertain of the extent of my powers, I stretched forth my hand and made the rain stop, not just over me but over the entire village and for some distance around it. I saw her pause with the sudden stopping of the rain and look around. Then, pushing her rain slicked hair back, she turned again to the task at hand, oblivious of the source of her good fortune. Rain still fell from the clouds above her head, but it did not touch the village. Instead it slid sideways across my magic barrier until it could once again fall to the ground.

Satisfied, I made my way down the hill to the village gate, designed more to keep the animals in than intruders out. Seeing me, my mother called to me as I closed the gate behind me. 'Did you catch the goat?'

I stopped short in my tracks. I had completely forgotten about the goat that had wandered off this morning. It had been the reason I was out in all the mud and muck when I had met the Djinn."

He paused then, still leaning against the lamppost, inside whatever this area was between instants. The people beyond stood frozen, unchanged despite the time that had passed since he began his story.

Although I was fascinated by his tale, my stomach chose that moment to growl loudly. "Uh... that's all fascinating." I said, before he could continue. "I don't mean to be rude, but you wouldn't happen to know about any food in this space, would you?" I gave a vague gesture to indicate the area he had created. "I was headed off to lunch when I saw you. I don't know about you but I'm just a little hungry. Could we continue this in a restaurant over some food?"

He blinked twice and moved away from the lampost, a look of what I took for genuine concern coming over his face. "Food... Of course, of course. Forgive me dear fellow. I sometimes get carried away. Don't have much chance to talk to folks these days you know. Now what would you like… Turkey, Ham, ah, I know…" and with the merest motion of his hand a table and two chairs appeared from nowhere. On the table were two place settings of some reddish china and two crystal glasses filled with an amber liquid. A platter of sliced meat and bread sat in the middle of the table. "Please, sit down and help yourself." he said as he sat and piled meat upon a slice of bread.

I was somewhat reluctant to trust food that had just appeared out of nowhere, but I was starving. Watching him devour his sandwich broke down any reservations I may have had, and I sat and reached for the bread and meat. I quickly made a huge sandwich with something that looked and smelled liked turkey and, banishing any last-minute doubts, took a bite. It was wonderful! The turkey was fresh and seasoned with some herbs that made me want to take a second bite before I had finished with the first. The bread held a hint of rye, but was a dark brown color that I was not familiar with. Regardless, it was WONDERFUL, and I ate quickly yet savoring every bite. Taking the glass in hand I sipped the liquid inside carefully and paused as the flavor of rich, ripe peaches spread across my tongue like wildfire before a summer breeze. I had never tasted anything like it and drank more, savoring every mouthful.

"This is all delicious." I said when once I paused from eating long enough to say anything.

He smiled with a modest, almost shy grin, seemingly genuinely pleased by my praise.

"I'm glad you like it. It's just something I threw together. Help yourself, there's plenty more where this came from."

I didn't need any more encouragement to indulge myself and we ate in silence until satisfied. Then we both sat back in our chairs and sipped more of the peach nectar. I could not help but marvel that although we had obviously been talking and eating for some time, it was just as he had said. Nothing beyond this space between the instants had changed. While swirling the nectar within my glass, I regarded the people frozen there and pondered how my view of the world had changed in such a short time.

"Dessert?" came the question from the other side of the table. "I know this wonderful Babylonian recipe. I've been dying to try it out. It's a mixture of Marzipan and fruit mixed in layers between this wonderful cake…"

"That sounds wonderful but I couldn't eat another bite right now. I haven't eaten this much in years. It was so good I just couldn't get enough. Maybe later? …"

"Ah, well maybe later then." He seemed a little disappointed but brightened at the compliment about lunch. Settling back in his chair, which somehow had become more full and plush, he started on his narrative again pausing occasionally to sip the peach nectar.

"Now where was I? Oh yes, I remember now, the goat. I had completely forgotten about it what with the Djinn and all. 'I'm sorry Mother, I began, but I didn't see the goat. Its tracks led a far distance from here but then they seemed to turn back towards here. I tried to follow, but the tracks disappeared in the mud.'

I could tell my mother was upset. She stood and turned her sun-darkened face to gaze beyond the village fence and I could see her dismay reflected in her eyes. She breathed a deep sigh.

'That was our best milk goat Elam. Now what am I supposed to do?'

We were poor as the dirt beneath our feet but I had never seen my mother seem so low. Seeking to reassure her I quickly said, 'I sure it will be all right. Its tracks were headed towards the village when they disappeared Mother. I'm sure it will show up soon.'

She sighed again and turned back to her work. 'I hope so Elam. We need its milk to make the cheese I promised your aunt I'd give her for your brother's clothes.'

I stood still as if listening and scanning the hill for signs of movement. In reality I was stretching forth my will to try and bring the goat home. I didn't realize that I was doing it until I had found the goat two hills over on the opposite side of the village from where I had been searching. Nudging it with my mind, I mentally started it back towards home while I began heading out to meet it.

'Don't worry Mother. I'll keep looking. I'll find it.'

'I hope so Elam. I certainly hope so.'

I met the goat on the far side of the hill and started to lead it back when it occurred to me what I had done. I had felt the goat while it was two hills away. I had FELT the goat! I stopped and paid closer attention to my thoughts and to what I was feeling. I DID feel the goat, but I also FELT my mother and the other villagers, and the trees, and the shrubs, and even the rest of the animals that roamed the enclosure now that the rain was no longer pushing them to find what shelter they could. I marveled at this and pondered it for the rest of the day as I went about the tasks my mother set for me.

As the days passed I experimented with my new powers, doing this and that, to see how things would work. I made it so the animals would not stray beyond a certain distance outside the fence. I cleared the sky of clouds so the sun would shine and dry the muddy ground. I changed the course of the nearby stream so my mother would not have so far to go to fetch water and I urged the flowers on the hill to bloom early for the sheer pleasure of seeing the color against the clear blue sky.

I grew more confident in my powers as I practiced and soon, I was doing more and more. Every time a villager would cast a net into the sea I would fill it with fish. When the crops were sown, I made them grow faster and more bountiful. When the land grew too dry, I would bring the rain until the land was content and green with growth. In short, the village prospered and grew in wealth and size attracting newcomers seeking a part of the plenty to be found there. The huts slowly were replaced by more substantial buildings, which spread beyond the confines of the now vanished fence.

Years passed, and with the new wealth came traders with wondrous goods and stories of the world beyond our hills and shoreline. One day, I got permission from my mother to travel with a merchant to a market in the nearest town, some days away. The trip opened my eyes to possibilities I had not dreamed of, and I was excited as I explored the marvels of the town and market. All too soon it was time to return home and I traveled quickly with the items bought, filled with dreams and stories to share with my family. The trip passed pleasantly and almost before I knew it I was gazing from the hill upon my village.

Little Book of Stories

I saw ruins. With a choked cry I scrambled down the hill and ran to where the burnt and crumbled embers of what had been buildings lay. Bodies lay where they had fallen, wounds no longer bleeding into the red stained dirt beneath them. I stumbled towards my home and found what I had feared. My mother and brother lay dead, prey like all the rest to whatever raiders had found the village a fat and unprotected prize. I tried to revive them. I tried to make them live again, but I could not. I did not know how. A limitation it would seem to all the power I now held.

Numb with grief, I lost all track of time. Even now I don't know how long I sat there holding my mother's lifeless body. I do remember the sun rising and waking me, from a fitful sleep filled with nightmares, to a reality that seemed carved from them. I buried the dead and left. I have never returned.

I searched for the raiders for some time without success. They might, I suppose, have come from the sea. I never found them. I used my power to keep me alive while I wandered, duplicating coins to buy food and shelter when near a town and creating food and drink when I was not.

I spent decades wandering thus. I spent time in different locales living with the people there for a while and then drifting on. I came to see that the more I used my power the easier it became and, the more I learned, the more I was able to do. Knowledge became an all-consuming passion. I would not be put in a position again where I would be helpless to change what had occurred. But I also became more aware of the unanticipated consequences of the use of my power.

If I changed the course of a river to help irrigate a valley, the land where it once had flowed withered and died. If I pushed the rain away from a region to let the crops ripen to perfection, the next nation over would suffer from floods and famine as their crops perished. If I "uncovered" a previously unknown vein of gold near a town, greed and envy would follow like the wind as people sought to carve their fortune at the expense of everyone else and rode roughshod over the workers digging their wealth from the ground.

I grew to see that every use of my power could have consequences far different from what I had originally intended. As the years passed, I began to grow cautious and more sparing in what I did. It took a very long time but now I've stopped doing almost anything that could be considered earthshaking and content myself with little things, like when you saw me stopping that girl from falling."

I nodded, not really understanding what he was saying. "Uh huh."

Content with my response he continued.

"I also didn't age or, if I did, it was at a rate so slow that no one could detect it. Consequently, I could not stay in one place for any long period of time and made it a habit of moving every ten years or so. Eventually, I discovered how to hide myself and my home in a fog of non-seeing, if you will. Then I could stay put for as long as I wanted and venture out to see the world without moving everything I had collected as well."

"Excuse me for asking this, but just how old are you anyway?"

"Oh thousands of years old my boy, thousands of years."

He paused to take a long drink of the peach nectar before continuing.

"Oh I've had companions along the way, but I could never give them the sort of longevity that I enjoy. It was always very painful to lose them, but I don't know how to stop that from happening. I've outlived everyone I've ever loved and my children and their children and their children by so many years that I don't even try to figure it out anymore."

He looked pained as he talked of this and saddened by the loss of those now vanished in the distant past. Trying to be sensitive but yet still curious I asked, "Couldn't you have given them power like yourself? Your immortality, if that's what it is, seems somehow to be connected to that."

He paused, and with a narrowing of his eyes regarded me more closely, slowly sipping more nectar before replying.

"I was a little slow on the uptake on that idea. It took a while for the isolation of what I had become to sink in. After the first two or three centuries, I eventually thought of trying to give someone else power so I could share my life. But it doesn't seem to work that way. You seem to have to have an affinity for this in the first place. To be on the doorstep so to speak before it can be opened up and all this power let through. I've tried countless times over the centuries but haven't once succeeded. Of course, there was this pretty little Numidian ... I did manage to extend her life for several decades, but even she eventually grew old and died. We did have fun though while it lasted."

He sighed wistfully and, holding the glass in both hands, stared off into the distance at something I could not see.

Reluctant to interrupt his thoughts, I sat there for a moment before venturing to speak.

"Excuse me, but with all this power at your disposal, why couldn't you grant someone the same power just like the Djinn gave it to you?"

He smiled sadly and nodded slowly.

"You would think it should be that easy wouldn't you. But it isn't. Remember that affinity I spoke of? The Numidian came from a very long-lived family. They had an affinity for long life. I was able to tweak that, so to speak, in order to keep her young far longer than would have normally been the case. But she had no affinity for this sort of thing."

He waved his hand and the table was clear of food and dishes. In their stead were candlesticks of wrought iron and fruit and cheese slices on large platters. I blinked at the transformation and reached for a wedge of what looked and smelled like Gouda.

"But why not? If you could extend her life span, why couldn't you give her power?"

He paused and grew more thoughtful and spoke again.

"Think of it like this. Take a bottle capable of holding one liter of liquid. Hook it up to a machine and force two liters into it. What will happen?"

"Well," I began, "I suppose that one of two things will happen. Either the machine will stop, not having enough pressure to force the liquid into the bottle, or the bottle will burst due to the pressure of trying to hold more than it can."

He reached for a slice of apple and bit into it, smiling slightly at the taste.

"Now what happens if you hook a balloon up to the machine instead of the bottle?"

Catching his meaning I replied, "It expands slowly until it can hold no more. Then if you push more past its limit, it too will burst."

He nodded. "Exactly. It is much the same with the power. It is like a great ocean of liquid slowly being pushed into a person. You must have a container big enough to hold it."

"Or flexible enough to expand over time to hold increasing amounts."

He nodded again. "That's right. I think you've grasped the concept very well. I cannot give the power to someone who does not have the capacity to absorb it so to speak, to flex and expand metaphysically as the power flows into them."

I thought on this for a moment, somehow troubled by his answer.

"But how... how can you know whether they have the required flexibility?"

He paused and took another piece of apple from a tray and then slowly leaned forward in his chair.

"They see me."

"They see you?"

"They see me."

"But what does that mean. You've been seen by millions. You've lived among them. You've eaten with them. You've learned from them, studied, married, and had children. You've been seen!"

He smiled and leaned back in his chair again.

"But not when I don't wish to be seen."

I stopped openmouthed as the implications rushed in. He munched contentedly upon his apple as I fumbled for words.

"The… the Djinn. You saw the Djinn."

He nodded encouragingly.

I sat back in my chair astonished at what this meant.

"The Djinn didn't grant your wish because of what you wanted but because you saw it. You were on the threshold and had the flexibility to hold the power. Your wish was secondary to the entire process."

"That's right, up to a point. I did see him. I was on the threshold. I could hold the power. But I also wanted to hold the power. Those four things existing at the same time in a person is extremely rare. If any of those ingredients had been missing, the Djinn would have been as powerless to grant my wish as I was in all those years of trying."

"So it takes all those things to allow you to give the power to someone."

"That's right."

"Oh." I said as it finally dawned on me what this was really all about. "And you said that occasionally someone sees you."

He nodded again. "Yes."

"And I saw you."

"Yes."

"So I have three of the four ingredients."

"Yes."

"All I have to do is decide if I want the power."

He leaned forward once again. "Yes."

The redhead's voice brought me back to the sounds of the fast food place. A low murmur of conversation hung in the air as she leaned forward, focused intently on me, her expression now tinged with a hint of... incredulity.

"You were right. That is quite a story. Not at all what I was expecting. So what did you do? Did you ask for the power? I know that I would have."

I turned and looked at her, once more aware of where I was as she continued.

"It would be so cool to have that kind of power. You could do anything, anything at all."

I looked at her with tired eyes and smiled wistfully.

Grieco

"Would it? Could you?" was all I said, suddenly very tired although it was only shortly after noon.

The world slowed to crawl as I stood up to leave, a look of surprise frozen in those soft brown eyes as I seemed to disappear. Suddenly having had enough of this place, I drank down the last of my shake and moved past a family of four who only a moment before had been happily fussing over a tray full of food. Reaching out, I gently adjusted the youngest in her chair, stopping her from accidentally knocking her meal to the floor.

Satisfied, I continued to the exit, pushing the door open and going outside to see what the rest of the day might bring.

Imprisoned though my spirit be

The bars of light called to him, pleaded for him to touch them, and when he did… there was music. Or perhaps not music really. There was no collection of notes, of words orchestrated into a cohesive moving piece with beginning and end. No. This seemed to flow in and around him. It melded with his soul and merged feelings and emotions and… everything… into a whole that could not be denied.

He soared and flew as his hands danced across the bars coaxing more light and sound into being, immersing himself until he did not know where it ended, and he began. There was no sense of time. He floated. A thousand years, a million could have passed and he would not have noticed so absorbed was he in the music. He was only dimly aware that there were others there as well, all around, all floating in whatever this was that held them as they touched the bars and were enveloped in sensation.

But even as the music held him, embraced him, surrounded him, there was still somehow a sense of disquiet. Something that marred the music and colored it in a way that jarred and caused discordant streams within the flow. He waved his hands to push them, to brush them away, to try and return to the music. But no matter how fast he waved, how wide his arms might reach, the discord remained, a blemish on the beauty that invaded his soul.

He tried one last time, reaching wide and then bringing his hands together quickly in one swift motion when he felt it, something thin and flexible yet at the same time hard beneath the spot where his hands touched. He stopped, remaining motionless, unwilling to lose whatever it was that rested there beneath his hands. And as the colored bars called and pleaded for him to resume, he ignored them, closing his hands around two thin strands. And then he pulled.

He felt something give and slide away through something in the center of his face. *His nose? What was this thing doing in his nose and…* Light washed over him, and he became aware that he was standing, held upright by a suspension rig that supported his frame in the middle of a small round enclosure. He felt, then saw the cables and intravenous tubes inserted into tabs on the thin formfitting skinsuit that covered his body. He was holding two thin fiber optic-like cables, one in each hand, and he stared as he fought to make sense of where this was, what this was.

A figure in white moved somewhere near his left side and a man's voice intruded on his muddled thoughts. "There, there, no need to be concerned. It sometimes takes a couple of times for someone to get adjusted to the environment. I'll have you reset in just a minute."

The environment? Had he heard correctly? What was this place? What was this get up and equipment he was in? Who was this man and why was he reassuring him about "the environment"?

"Almost there." The man's voice came again as a yellow light flashed softly on a panel overhead. "Just a couple of seconds now. You'll begin to feel more relaxed as the sedative takes effect and then I'll reinsert those tubes."

Sedative? His hands began to relax in spite of his efforts to keep them clenched around the cables. He felt them being eased away from him and then a slight pressure as something was gently inserted through the openings of his nose. He felt it on the left side first with a kind of tingling sensation as a connection was made between the living fibers of the cable and… something deep inside. *Neural connection,* his mind faintly told him as the second cable was inserted and connection made and… the bars of light called to him, pleaded for him to touch them, and when he did… there was music…

☐

He could not say how long he touched the bars, how long the music enveloped him, penetrated him, and washed him clean with its beauty. He only knew that somehow, just there, at the edge of his perception, at the very boundaries of his soul, the discord remained. It nagged at him. It intruded on his peace. It spoke to him in a way the music could not. He did not want it and yet it lingered despite the soaring tones, despite the quickness of his hands upon the bars, in spite of his best efforts to ignore it and to push it away.

And yet, somewhere deep in his mind he kept hearing two words he came to associate with the eddy of discord within the music flow. *Neural connection.* His hands faltered as he strove to capture the meaning of those words, the music losing strength and becoming muddied as gaps developed in the flow around him. Unbidden, the memory of cables being inserted flashed like lightning in his mind and he knew, knew that this was somehow wrong, that the music was a trap, a ruse to keep him tranquil and oblivious to whatever waited beyond this… place.

His hands stopped and came together as though seeking rest, a simple pause in the constant touching of the bars. And when they did, he felt it, that sense of something there, thin and flexible, waiting to be grasped and pulled…

His eyes opened and he blinked to clear the blurry image of the enclosure he was once more in. He glanced to his left and saw a line of folk in enclosures just like his, all moving their arms and hands in the same intricate dance that he too had just been involved in. When he looked right, the same was true. A light in the panel above him flashed a soft yellow as a mechanical voice sounded from a speaker sited there "Cube Beta 1578. Status Yellow." The fiber cables fell from his hands as he tried desperately to reconcile this with the place he had just emerged from.

By the second growing more alert, he quickly began pulling cables and tubes from connections on whatever this was he was wearing. Ridding himself of them, he then worked as quickly as he could to undo the latches in the rig that suspended him in the center of... this place. Once freed and on the floor, he staggered as his legs refused at first to take the weight of his body after being suspended for so long. He leaned against the frame of what passed for a doorway into this enclosure... *no*... *Cube*... for that was what the gently insistent voice kept saying as the light began flashing red "Cube Beta 1578. Status Red."

Yellow. Red. It didn't quite make sense but somehow, he knew that it had something to do with his breaking away from those cables and tubes. He shook his head, trying desperately to clear it. He could feel his strength returning but his mind was still a muddle, racing to try and make sense of where he was. *Prison. That was it. He was in prison.* Though for what he still had no...

He heard the sound of a door closing somewhere. As the sound faded, echoing slowly against unseen walls somewhere in the distance, he looked around frantically for something to use against whoever was coming. He moved around the cube, pushing and pulling at panels and doors in the half wall that comprised the lower portion of the cube. Only one opened but it held nothing but some pamphlets extolling the virtues of the virtual prison system. *Virtual prison.* That explained the lights and the music. He'd been imprisoned in virtual reality with the fiber cables making a neural connection directly with the frontal cortex of his brain. *He was a prisoner. None of it was real. None of it...*

The sound of footsteps drawing near brought him back to his immediate situation. With nowhere to go, he quickly lay on the floor of the cube, one hand grasping one of the cables dangling from the ceiling. With any luck it would look as though he had collapsed after working himself free of the suspension gear.

"Son of a..." a male figure, dressed in a white lab coat over street clothes, stepped quickly into the cube. Stopping briefly to bend over and check for life signs, the man stood and turned to a raised panel just below the flashing light. "Why do I always get the troublemakers? Charlie spends all day here and never gets even a hint of a problem. But me, I'm on shift for twenty minutes and..." With a snort of exasperation he pressed the button below the light silencing the voice. He leaned forward towards a hidden microphone in the panel. "Cube Beta 1578. Proctor Oscar Thomas clearing red status. Process underway." He pressed the button again and started to turn back to his problem for the day. Unfortunately for him, that problem was no longer lying on the floor.

A slim flexible cable flashed by the Proctor's face to quickly tighten around his throat, making it increasingly hard to breathe. He grabbed for the cable with both hands, trying desperately to get at least one under it, to somehow ease the pressure as he fought for air. His vision became blurry, then dim, as he sank towards the blackness that rose to swallow him.

The prisoner felt the Proctor go limp and sag backwards against him. Lowering him to the floor, the prisoner quickly checked for a pulse. Finding one, he rapidly searched through the pockets of the lab coat for anything that that might help him now. Thrusting his hand into the right pocket, his fingers brushed against a smooth, thin object. Closing his hand around it, he drew it from the pocket, pausing to read the label that helpfully marked the syringe as a Class A Sedative. He stared at it for a moment, trying to remember all the shots he must have been given as he was growing up. All he managed to get was a dim recollection of alcohol swabs against his right shoulder and some sort of injection being given. *Flu shot* a faint voice inside his head told him. *Probably the best way to do it…* Kneeling down next to the Proctor, he maneuvered the man's arms out of the lab coat. *Have to get access to his arm…* Rolling the Proctor over onto his back, he started to unbutton the shirt… *cotton…* when the flickering of the man's eyelids told him he'd nearly run out of time.

Pulling the plastic protective cap off the end of the syringe, the prisoner looked frantically for someplace to use it in the skin area he'd managed to uncover thus far. *The neck… quick the neck…* He drove the needle into the Proctor's neck trying not to push it too far in yet not having the luxury of being able to be too careful. "What…" The Proctor managed to gasp as he started to become conscious before slipping rapidly into oblivion as the sedative took effect. Recapping the syringe, the prisoner leaned back in relief for a moment, considering his situation before tossing it aside and beginning to undress the Proctor, placing each item in a pile on the floor on top of the lab coat.

Finished, he started working on the formfitting skinsuit he was wearing. *How does this thing… Ah…There it is…* He slid his fingers under a tab by his left shoulder and felt it slide free, suddenly opening an easily missed seam down the entire left side of the suit. He half peeled, half pulled it off and started to toss it aside. He stopped in mid-motion as the slowly flashing red light once more penetrated his conscious mind. *Wait… I'll need this… Have to reset that somehow…* He looked around the cube, his eyes coming to rest on the prone body of the Proctor. *They can't search for me if they don't know I'm gone... But first...* He reached over to the pile of the Proctor's clothes and quickly sorted through them... *They look about the right size...* and started to dress. Once done, he turned to the task of getting the Proctor into the skinsuit.

Harder than I thought it'd be... he thought to himself as he pushed and pulled the Proctor one way and then the other trying to get the suit past the knees and up over the abdomen. *Good thing this suit has some stretch to it...* Finally, he maneuvered the Proctor's arms into the sleeves of the suit. Done, he pushed the tab into place on the shoulder of the suit and watched the seam vanish as the suit sealed.

The prisoner rested for a moment as he considered what to do next. *Have to get him into that rig somehow...* Standing, he walked over to the suspension rig and examined the connections and clasps he'd have to attach to the suit. Satisfied that at least he had some idea how to proceed, he moved back to where the Proctor lay. Bending down, he grabbed him under the arms and dragged him across to the center of the rig.

This guy's heavy... Well there's no other way... Dropping the Proctor for a moment, the prisoner grabbed him around the waist and tried to lift him to where he'd be able to fasten the skinsuit to the suspension rig. He struggled with the weight of the Proctor, trying to shift him to one arm so he could grab the rig with the other. *No use... He's just too heavy...* He lowered the Proctor's limp form to the floor and stepped outside the rig to look for some other way to get this done.

He walked around the Cube, once more pulling and pushing on draws and doors to see if he could find anything that might be of use. Again only the drawer with the pamphlets opened at his touch. He pulled a handful out trying to see if maybe, just maybe there was something else hidden there. *Nothing*... He started to toss them aside when one caught his eye. *Bayside... Seems like a nice place...* He absentmindedly placed the pamphlet in the left pocket of the lab coat while he continued to search the Cube.

There's got to be something... His eyes stopped at the panel where the light still flashed a soft red. *That... Proctor... was doing something over there...* Drawing close, he looked across the dials and gauges. *Blood pressure... calcium level... flow rate...* He stopped at one that showed a line, now flat and level, moving from left to right on a seemingly constantly refreshing inset screen. *Neural engagement...* He paused for a second, glancing back at the Proctor to make sure he showed no sign of rousing, then continued on across the panel finally finding a rocker switch that was simply labeled 'Suspension Rig'.

What the hell... Nothing else seems to be connected with that thing. He reached up and pulled the rocker switch downward. Behind him he heard a mechanical whir as the rig slowly lowered. He glanced back and watched it descend until most of the rig's harness was lying on the floor, on and around the motionless Proctor. Releasing the switch, he turned back and moved over to the rig, picking it up and moving the harness from one hand to the other until he found latches that looked like they connected to each side of the suit.

Let's see if this works... He knelt next to the Proctor and worked with the latches trying them on each side of the suit until he found the ones that seemed to fit. *Well at least they seem to connect... that's a start.* He walked back to the panel and moved the rocker switch up. The whir sounded again as the suspension rig began to rise towards the ceiling, slowly dragging the Proctor into an upright position. Once the Proctor's feet cleared the ground, the Prisoner let go of the switch and moved to stand next to the now suspended form. He leaned in to examine the markings on the tabs located on the arms and the front of the suit. *Color coded...* He moved around the rig, gathering cables and tubes as he went, matching the color on the end of each to the matching color on the tabs. Each seated with a distinctive 'snap' as he pushed them home. As he connected the last tube to the suit, the light on the panel changed to yellow. "Cube Beta 1578. Status Yellow." came the voice from the panel speaker.

Must be doing something right... Now where are those two neural cables?... Ah, there they are... He walked around the Proctor's suspended form and collected the two remaining cables, thin and flexible, in his hands as he moved back to the Proctor. *No color code here... wonder if it matters which side they go in... only one way to find out.* He moved to the Proctor, gently maneuvering the man's head back so he had easy access to his nose. *Left side first...* He remembered the sensation of the cable sliding up and in, with the living fiber doing the rest to connect somehow. *Here goes nothing.*

He looked at the cables again, trying to see something, anything to guide him. Shrugging, he finally just chose the one in his right hand and slid it slowly up and into the Proctor's left nostril. The fiber cable moved easily, almost as though lubricated, though he felt nothing but the cable's surface as he pushed. *How far does this thing go...* The cable moved suddenly in his hand, almost like a snake striking its prey, and then began to pulse with a rhythmic beat as man and machine became connected. *Damn... so that's what happens...* He took the second cable and inserted it in the right side of the Proctor's nose, doing the same as he had with the other until this cable also almost leapt from his hand as it sought and made the neural connection deep inside. Both cables pulsed, in sync with wherever it was that the Proctor's mind now was. On the panel the light changed to a soothing blue and the voice came once again. "Cube Beta 1578. Status Blue. Fault cleared." The prisoner felt himself relax as the change provided confirmation that he had managed to get it right.

Now to get out of here... He came through a door somewhere out there. The prisoner moved from the Cube into the relative darkness of the area outside. He stood a moment letting his eyes adjust to the dimmer lighting. Once that happened, he looked at the corridors stretching out in all directions from where he stood. At even intervals, the darkness was interrupted by pools of light that spilled out from other enclosures spread out into the distance as far as he could see. *Damn... This is a big place... Wonder how many of these Cubes there are?... Now which way did that sound come from? Maybe I should just walk until I find a wall.* After one more look down seemingly identical corridors, he chose a direction and began to walk.

□

It was hard to tell how long he'd walked past one Cube after another, their occupants all moving in the same motions, reaching and touching something that wasn't there, at least here in the real world. They were all different; men, women, some younger, some older, but all completely captured by the sounds and the colors of the music that he, thankfully, was free of. He'd almost given up hope of ever reaching a wall when the line of Cubes suddenly just stopped. He almost walked past the last one without noticing but managed to catch himself and stop before moving beyond. He stood there examining the readouts on a panel outside the Cube, spending some time trying to make sense of the information shown there. *Cube Beta 19,999...* The occupant showed no signs of noticing, continuing to move her arms in the intricate choreography endemic to the Cubes. *Too bad... she's pretty... no, more than that...* He shook his head, amused that he could think of such things when getting out of... here... should be his only concern. A subtle brightening marked a walkway just beyond the Cube and a sign hung where a wall should have been but somehow wasn't. Numbers and a set of arrows told of Cube numbers to the right (Alpha 10,001 - 20,000) and to the left (Alpha 10,000 – 0, Zeta 0 - 10,000).

Just like in a hotel... Too bad there's no exit sign. He rubbed his face with his hands thinking hard but unsure of what to do next. *That's an awful lot of Cubes. The door could be anywhere.* "So how do I find the way out?" He stopped, surprised at the sound of his voice and the echoes of the words that slowly faded in the maze of Cubes. He was equally surprised when the voice he'd last heard in his Cube came from the panel he'd just been examining. "The exit is located to your left across from Cube Alpha 6999. It is marked by a green arrow in the floor of the walkway." *Son of a... All I had to do was ask?* The prisoner eased his head out from the edge of the Cube, glancing each way along the corridor. Satisfied that he was alone, he moved out into the center of the walkway and turned left.

It wasn't too long before he found himself standing on a green arrow in the walkway looking at a closed door. *Still no exit sign... and no doorknob... just a handle to pull it open with.* He reached for the handle and gave it a tug. *Nothing... closed tight... must be a way to open it somewhere around here.* He moved back a bit and examined the door. It was a plain rectangle with no distinguishing features except for the handle and the green tint that marked its surface. However, mid-way up on the right side of the frame, there was a raised square of dark material with a red light in the center of its surface. He put his hand on it, covering the surface, momentarily blocking the light. *Well it was worth a try… Maybe it's some sort of card reader…* He reached into the pockets of the street clothes, pulling out the contents and looking through them before returning them one by one to where he'd found them. *Gum… some sort of hard candy… keys… wallet…* He opened it and perused the contents. *Credit cards… some money… temporary driver's license…* He closed and pushed the wallet back into the right front pocket of his borrowed pants. *Nothing to help me with this…*

So… maybe not a card reader… maybe a badge reader of some kind… He reached down into the left pocket of the lab coat, feeling for anything that might be a badge. He felt something squarish and soft and pulled it out. *A sandwich of some sort…* He opened the plastic wrap that held it and ventured a sniff. *Ham?* He took a small bite and rolled the piece around on his tongue for taste. *Yeah ham… and some sort of mustard…* Pleased, he wrapped the sandwich back up and put it back in the pocket for later. As he did, his fingers brushed against something thin and hard just below where the sandwich had previously been. *Ah ha! What's this?* Retrieving it, he found it to be a simple laminated badge attached to a broken lanyard. The face of the Proctor looked out from its surface above a barcode and some numbers which meant nothing to him. *Maybe this will do it.* He held the barcode of the badge up to the reddish light and was rewarded with a loud click from the door. Taking this as his cue, he grabbed the handle and gave it a pull, feeling it give and smoothly open towards him. After a quick look at the room beyond, he let go and stepped through, letting the door close behind him.

Some sort of staff area… He walked around the medium sized, comfortably appointed spaces. He tried out the cushions on a couch with his hand… *Must be comfortable…* before completing his survey. *Lounge… kitchenette… bathroom… shower area… lockers…* He stopped in front a row of six lockers. Only two had names mounted above their doors. He tried the one labeled Oscar Thomas. *Hmmm. No lock. Let's see what's inside.* He pulled items out one at a time laying them down on a bench bolted to the floor immediately in front the lockers. *Jacket… scrubs…must not have had time to change before my alarm went off… boots…* He held them up, examining them, then put the bottom of one against the bottom of his left foot. *About my size… could come in handy.* Putting them to one side, he continued to rummage through the locker. *Lunch box… real estate brochure… hmmm.* He turned it over in his hands, opening it to reveal a floor plan and interior of a house the Proctor might have been considering. A note in pen was scribbled in the margin of the brochure. "This could be the one. Call agent in the morning to set up a walk through. Now if only I had someone to share cost." *Must be single if he needed someone to help out buying it… 123 South Ruger St, Bayside… No wonder that brochure was in the drawer back in my Cube.* He put the brochure aside to look at later and returned the rest to the locker.

Moving to his left, he read the name on the second labeled locker. *Charlene Roberts… that's got to be the 'Charlie' the Proctor was talking about when he started to clear my red status. I wonder…* He opened her locker and rifled through its contents. *Nothing out of the ordinary here… Wait. What's that?…* There in the back of the locker shelf was a book-like object. He pulled it out and opened it, looking through what lie inside. *A scrapbook? No, more of a photo album with newspaper items added in.* He turned the pages and the faces of strangers, captured in a moment of happiness at the beach, a birthday party, high school graduation, peered out of each sheet. *Always just the three of them… her parents and her I suppose.* He continued turning, each photo a revelation, each article a tidbit about the other Proctor who would be back in... *about 10 and half hours if Oscar's shift started at noon.*

The last page of the book held an article from what must have been her hometown newspaper. It told the story of a car crash on a winter's day, across an icy road and through the guardrail to the steep ravine beyond. The occupants, a man and a woman, were both killed instantly. *Her parents...* An obituary pasted to the bottom of the same page confirmed the thought. He closed the book and returned it to where he'd found it, the seeds of an idea just starting to take hold. *What are the odds that...* He reached into the locker and removed a pair of scrubs much like the ones in Oscar's locker but different in size and color. With scrubs in hand, he made his way back to the staff lounge door, opened it, and, turning left, made his way back into the maze of Cubes.

He spent the next seven hours exploring and checking out the maze. The Cubes were all identical except for their occupants. The rows indistinguishable except for the numbers that marked each one and the signs at the end of each row. He found an office area, a combination of medical bay, laboratory, and administrative spaces, like a central hub in the middle of the maze, tying it all together. Storage cabinets opened at a touch of the Proctor's badge and he took the opportunity to put several syringes, containing a variety of sedatives, in the pockets of the lab coat. He had three of the Class A, but also pocketed a few potentially less potent drugs... just in case.

The admin area was a bureaucrat's dream with cameras, badge and card makers, and files on past and present Proctors. He spent some time reading through Oscar's and Charlie's personnel files, gleaning every last tidbit about family members, (there were no immediate family), education, financial info, birth certificates, and personal histories. Then he gave himself a crash course on running the badge maker and managed to do a credible job of replacing the Proctor's badge with one that featured his face above Oscar Thomas's information. Despite giving himself a slight burn on his hand, he even managed to get his new badge laminated and to string a new lanyard through the machine punched hole at the top. Then, once satisfied that he'd done all he could, he headed back through the maze to the staff lounge where he settled in to wait.

□

Charlie showed up a few minutes early for her shift. Closing the outer door behind her, she called out "Hey Oscar, I decided to give you a break and get here early for a change." She moved deeper into the staff lounge while pulling off the light jacket she'd worn to keep off the night chill. Getting no response and with the lounge apparently empty, she assumed Oscar was dealing with something out in the Cubes. "Hope he doesn't leave me a mess to clean up. If it started on his shift, he's supposed to deal with it." Throwing her coat on the couch, she moved over to the kitchenette, enticed by the smell of coffee.

"Well at least he made some joe." She poured herself some after opening an overhead cabinet and taking down a mug. She took a sip, savoring the flavor. "Damn. This is better than his usual brew. That boy's learning." After another sip, she put the mug down on the counter and walked into the locker area. "Might as well get ready for work." Opening the locker she reached in and stopped when her hand met only air. "I could have sworn I left a set of scrubs in there. If Oscar's been messing with my stuff, I'll tear him a new one when he gets back here." As she closed the locker, she caught a glimpse of white in the corner of her eye and started to turn. "It's about time you got here ..."

Grieco

She felt a sharp stinging sensation in her neck and her words stopped abruptly as her body went limp and a dark swirling pool rushed up to greet her.

☐

It all went pretty much to plan. Once Charlie had been sedated, the prisoner slung her over one shoulder and carried her out of the lounge and down the walkway to Cube Beta 19,999. Charlie's scrubs still lay on the floor where he'd left them after seeing that they were the right size, or close enough, to fit the female prisoner still moving to the unseen light and music of "the environment". Laying Charlie down against the inside wall of the Cube, he moved over to where its occupant was suspended in her rig. With some trepidation he took hold of the neural cables and gently pulled on them until he felt them disengage from deep inside. Then he pulled them more quickly, swiftly getting them away from her face.

She awakened quickly, bewildered at first by the change from where she'd been to where she found herself now. It took some time to orient her to the reality of the prison and the situation that they both were in. But once she was fully awake and alert, he explained his plan. They could both escape, but only if they did so together. He talked about what he'd learned, about Bayside, the house, and how they could, provided she agreed, buy it together, hiding under the identities of the Proctors. They could continue to work here, wherever that was, until their covers were firmly in place. Then they could give notice and simply walk away, building new lives for themselves out in the real world. They'd work the details out together as they went along. Of course, if she preferred to stay here, he could just put the cables back in and she could return to the lights and the music. No harm, no foul, and no risk to her.

She thought about it, but only for a moment, before croaking out her assent with a voice rusty with disuse. He used the rocker switch on the Cube's panel to lower her to the floor before quickly removing the tubes and cables from the tabs in her skinsuit and unhooking her from the rig itself. He stripped Charlie of her clothes while the woman prisoner removed the skinsuit. Once done, they reversed the process with the woman dressing in the Proctor's clothes while he worked to pull the skinsuit over Charlie's inert form. Then they worked together to hook Charlie to the suspension rig, connecting the color-coded cables and tubes to the matching tabs, and raising the rig until it held Charlie suspended above the Cube's floor. Finally, they slid the neural cables slowly into her nasal cavities until they felt the living fiber take hold and seat themselves. Almost immediately, Charlie's hands began to move, reaching for the bars of light that they, thankfully, could no longer see.

They spent the rest of Charlie's shift doing the immediate things; making a badge for the woman, letting her learn as much as possible about the Proctor and her life, and planning for the near future. They'd become boy and girlfriend. It was a logical thing to happen with them both being Proctors at the prison. It was reasonable that they might have become close, maybe even sharing shifts to pass the time and ease the loneliness. Of course, they'd both need new IDs. Working twelve hour shifts at the prison would have kept them mostly isolated from the community. Few if any would really know anything about them. The birth certificates from the personnel files would help in getting the documents they'd need to move freely in the outside world. And renting and then maybe later buying the house in Bayside would give their identities a solid base on which to build. Later, when they gave their notices, they could move away with confidence that they could escape from here unnoticed with the real Oscar and Charlie safely

Grieco

housed in Cubes in their place. As they talked, it became clear to both of them that they would make a good team, that this could really work on so many different levels.

☐

Elsewhere, the wall of a control center was filled by a bank of monitors. Displayed on almost all were constantly changing images of people floating in some sort of clear liquid in transparent cubes. No cables, tubes, or restraints of any kind were attached to the people inside. Only a soft, pliant cap was fastened to each person's head by a simple elastic strap. In the center of this cap, a single, thick fiber cable was attached, pulsing gently as data flowed to and from a central processing system located somewhere beyond view.

An older gentleman, wearing a badge that marked him as a VIP, leaned towards a central, large monitor that currently displayed the image of the escaped prisoners in the staff lounge. Looking away, he gazed with interest at what was shown on the other monitors. After a moment, he turned to his guide, "Those folks in the cubes... they don't appear to be breathing. Does the liquid in the cubes have something to do with that?"

His guide, standing with him as they watched the shifting scenes, nodded as he replied. "Yes it does. The liquid is infused with oxygen. There is a bit of an initial automatic reflex as the lungs fill up, but, once that instinctive reaction has passed, the liquid passes oxygen directly to the body using the normal processes of the lungs. When we breathe, oxygen enters the alveoli, or small air sacs in the lungs. Oxygen diffuses from there into the bloodstream. This liquid takes the place of the air we breathe but the oxygen gets transferred in much the same way."

Little Book of Stories

The VIP turned back to the larger screen, watching as the man lay down on the couch apparently settling in to sleep while the woman opened what seemed to be a manual for Cube operations and began to read. "And what's the story with these two? Are you just going to let them get away with what they did?"

The guide smiled, moving closer to the monitor. "I can see why you might think that. In actuality, they're both still held safe and sound in one of the cubes shown in the other monitors."

The VIP snorted, gesturing at the center display, "Well if that's the case, what's this charade all about then?"

His guide thought for a moment before responding. "Let me put it this way. Every once in a while, the subconscious of one of our inmates rebels at the virtual environment that they're immersed in. At some level that we haven't figured out yet, and they certainly aren't conscious of, they become aware that this…", he gestured at the wall of monitors, "is not real. That what they're experiencing in the virtual environment just doesn't make sense somehow. What you're seeing on the center screen is a case of our primary failsafe kicking in. In this case, the male prisoner's mind somehow recognized the environment he's been in as false. To prevent cognitive disruption, the program works with him to fashion a reality that allows him to restore belief that what he sees and does is real."

"And the whole escape thing?"

"Was his way of restoring his reality to a level that was acceptable to him."

The VIP gestured towards the middle screen. "Why the woman?"

Grieco

The guide shrugged; a gesture meant to impart that some things are just unknowable. "She was beginning to edge towards cognitive disruption. Not quite to the point that he had reached, but close enough that merging their VR into a single story seemed the correct path. They both subconsciously needed to escape where they were. This shared story, if you will, gives them both the escape they needed to stabilize within their cubes."

"Imprisoned though my spirit be, I am, within, myself." The VIP muttered, almost to himself.

"What's that sir?"

The VIP looked away from the screen, still musing. "Oh nothing really. Just a poem I once read. Seems appropriate somehow. Especially the last lines. 'So it is that I await, like a bird, within my soul to be set free.'"

"Interesting... though I'm not quite sure what it means."

"Oh, I don't know. I suppose it speaks to how no matter what form of prison we may find ourselves in, the human spirit will somehow find a way to endure, to wait its chance to break free from what has imprisoned it. Like these two." He motioned to the screen. "Makes you wonder though."

"Sir?"

"You know... all of this. It makes you wonder,"

"I'm not sure what you mean sir."

"Come on. After being surrounded by all this, don't you ever wonder if maybe you're just another one of those folks in a cube somewhere and that this..." He waved his hands in the air meaning everything here and beyond where they stood. "is just your failsafe fallback to prevent... what did you call it?"

"Cognitive disruption."

"Right. Cognitive disruption. How would you ever know that all this isn't some sort of fancy VR prison just like the one you're running here?"

The guide smiled again, shuffling somewhat awkwardly as he considered this possibility. "Well, maybe that's the point."

"What?"

"Does it really matter if what we see and feel and do every day is real or not as long as we think it is? I mean, we all make our own reality with all the choices we make and the things that we do or don't do. It's really no different for the folks inside those cubes. They can choose to touch the bars of light and embrace the music environment... or not and then, like our two escapees, craft a reality more acceptable to them, more to their liking. Are we really any different just because their world is VR and ours is real?"

The VIP shook his head and laughed, just a little. "I suppose you're right son. It probably doesn't matter a hill of beans... as long as we think it's real." He paused for a moment, glancing back at the two escapees still featured on the center monitor before turning back to the guide. "Well then... why don't we get on with the rest of the tour. What's next?"

"Of course sir. Next on the tour is a look at the medical transfer bay, the place where prisoners are brought for acclimation to the cube environment. It's really fascinating to see..." The sound of his voice disappeared as they walked from the control room into the hallway beyond. On the large display, the woman looked over at the man sleeping on the couch in the staff lounge. She moved over to where he lay, picking up a throw blanket from where it had been draped over the back of another chair. She opened the throw, placing it on the man carefully so as not to wake him. She lingered just a moment, lightly brushing back an unruly lock of hair that threatened to fall across his face, and she smiled.

As though on cue, the center display in the control room went blank, shifting the scene with the man and woman to one of the smaller screens upon the wall. Then, once the sensors in the room confirmed that no one was there to watch them, those screens turned off, in turn, one by one. Finally, even the overhead lights went off, leaving the room in a darkness interrupted only by the glow of a gently blinking blue light set into a panel in the middle of the wall. It pulsed softly in the dark, reassuring anyone who happened to see that everything was just as it was supposed to be.

Electroceuticals

Pain will break a person.
Pleasure will make them serve you forever.

Inside a small conference room in an unobtrusive facility located in a secluded spot somewhere deep in the countryside, the Director of Electroceutical Medical Devices (DEMD), welcomes the distinguished Senator chairing the Intelligence Oversight Subcommittee on Special Projects.

"Ah, Senator Thomas. On behalf of the entire EMD team let me say it's a real pleasure to have you here today! We are always glad to welcome members of the Oversight Subcommittee to our little part of the world. I think you'll find everything to your liking."

"Well, we'll see about that Mr. Williams. There are several of us on the committee that have expressed grave concerns over the things we've been hearing about your operation here. We've received some disturbing reports about unsanctioned experimentation that has raised serious questions about the nature of your work. ... That's why I'm here today, to get a first-hand look at your facility and get a better understanding of exactly what you're up to."

"Yes, I see. Well, we're an open book here at EMD. I hope to put your mind at ease during today's tour of the facility. I'll be happy to answer any questions you might have about our work. ... But first things first. Coffee? Arabica, I believe, two sugars, no cream?"

"I see your people have you well informed."

"Actually, it was your assistant who reached out to us as part of setting the schedule for today. I hope it's to your liking? …"

The senator takes a sip and then a deeper swallow. "That's perfect." *Smiles* "Usually, I can't get a decent cup of coffee if I don't make it myself. Kudos to your staff for managing to get this right."

"I'll be sure to pass that on. And please… call me Ted. *(Smiles)* Whenever anyone calls me Mr. Williams, I always have to look around to see if maybe my father is in the room."

"Ok then… Ted." *Takes another swallow of coffee.* "Why don't we get down to the business of today. I have to admit that I never was one for chit chat."

"Of course. Let me start with a brief description of the type of work we do here."

Ted takes a small device out of his pocket and clicks a button on it to start a PowerPoint presentation already running on a laptop on the conference table. A projector, also on the table, turns on and displays the first slide with the words 'Welcome Senator Thomas' on a large, built-in screen on the other side of the room. Ted periodically clicks the handheld device to change slides as he makes his presentation.

"I'll be fairly brief here Senator. The basic concepts involved in our work are pretty simple. I'll keep this at a high level and try not to dive down into too many technical details. We can talk more about it as we do the tour and go down to any level of detail that you'd like at that time. This presentation is an overview of sorts, designed to give the basic elements behind electroceuticals."

Ted pauses to see if this is agreeable to the Senator. When, after another swallow of coffee, the Senator nods his understanding, Ted continues.

"The nervous system is a critical part of the human anatomy. It transmits electrical signals governing every function of the body billions of times every second. We could not function if those signals were interrupted or stopped for any reason. Various neurodegenerative diseases inhibit or block those signals with disastrous results for the afflicted individuals. But for most folk, the nervous system functions just fine, controlling muscle and organ functions, warning us of danger or damage through pain, or rewarding us with pleasant sensations when we encounter stimuli that we find pleasing.

As this chart shows, the nervous system is one big superhighway running throughout the body. It branches off to smaller and smaller roads and streets as it runs from the brain through the central nervous system and off to the skin and extremities like our hands and feet. The basic approach of electroceuticals is to harness that highway by supplying electrical stimulation to alter the body's perception of things such as pain and to improve organ function in cases where the nervous system is somehow inhibited or otherwise causing improper function.

For example, an amputee may experience phantom pain from a missing limb. This sensation of pain is sometime caused by the clumping of nerves, that continue to grow after amputation, into a neuroma which generates a pain response. Early efforts to control this involved implanting a device in the patient, which they could control, to block those pain signals thus granting temporary relief. Other efforts sought to use the vagus nerve, shown here, to gain access to a broader set of bodily functions since it's a main pathway from the brain and branches off… merging, if you will, with smaller nerves to control various functions in the body. … Any questions so far Senator?"

Senator Thomas takes another sip of his coffee before responding. "No. It all seems fairly clear at this point. Please go on."

Ted clicks on the handheld device and moves on to the next slide. "The trouble with the latter approach is that it depended on a comprehensive, or at least fairly complete, mapping of the vagus nerve and its various offshoots and branches. Without that map, and the knowledge of which branch, which connections, did what, anything one tried would be pretty much hit and miss."

The Senator nods. "I can see how that would be a problem. Without a good understanding of the entire network, one might do more harm than good once they started trying electrical stimulation to manipulate the nervous system."

"Exactly. Most of the early efforts were stymied by the lack of an adequate map as well as by the large size of devices that were available to provide the electrical impulses. In order to truly integrate any device into the nervous system, it would have to be small enough to interface with the particular nerve that controlled the function one was attempting to influence or control. Fortunately, we have achieved huge progress in both of those areas.

The Stimulating Peripheral Activity to Relieve Conditions (SPARC) project was funded by the National Institutes of Health. One of SPARC's aims was to map out the nervous system, identifying every nerve, and its function, in the body outside the brain. EMD has successfully built on their work to the extent that we are now able to target specific nerves in the body to achieve desired outcomes."

The Senator finishes off the last of his coffee and crumples the paper cup, tossing it towards a wastebasket just off to the side near the door to the conference room. "Damn. I should have made that. I was all-state in basketball in high school. You'd think I'd be able to get a cup into a trashcan."

Ted smiles, giving a small chuckle at the Senator's plight. "Don't worry about it Senator. I'll grab it when we leave. Consider it an assist. … Did you have a question?"

"Yes. Yes, I did. You said there were two problems that had to be overcome. You seem to have managed to get your map, but don't you still need to get devices small enough to interface with the individual nerves?"

"That's correct Senator. Fortunately, however, we've made major strides in that area as well. We've harnessed advancements in nanotechnology and made some major breakthroughs ourselves in that area. We've managed to create incredibly small nanobots that, once introduced into the body, essentially fuse with the nerves themselves allowing us to stimulate specific nerves to achieve simply incredible results. I'll be showing you some of the results we've managed to get during the tour."

(Senator Thomas pushes his chair back and stands up.) "Well then, if you've finished your presentation, why don't we get on with the tour then."

Grieco

"Absolutely Senator. Right this way." *(Ted walks to the door of the conference room, picking up the discarded coffee cup and dropping it in the trashcan as he passes. He opens the door and ushers the Senator out.)* "After you, Senator."

Little Book of Stories

□

Ted and Senator Thomas are in a largish room equipped as a laboratory. Several employees dressed in lab clothing sit at various workstations accomplishing tasks on computers. Some peer into microscopes or watch images from similar devices displayed on monitors. Ted leads the Senator to one of the workstations equipped with a large display showing activity apparently captured from a petri dish located under a microscope's optics.

"Senator, if you'll come this way, I'd like to show you what we've managed to achieve in our research at the cellular level. At this workstation, we've introduced some of our latest nanobots into a cultured medium including nerve cells."

The Senator leans closer to the monitor to get a better look. "Are those little moving things the nanobots you're talking about?"

"Yes Senator, they are. Our bioengineers have managed to create nanobots that are programmed … that might not be exactly the correct word, but it describes what motivates the nanobots to accomplish what they're designed to do."

The Senator looks up from the monitor at Ted. "And what is that exactly?"

Ted pauses for just a moment as though searching for the right words to describe the process. After a moment's delay, he nods and replies. "You remember how I told you earlier that the nanobots are designed to be able to directly interface with the nerves in the body?" *He watches for the Senator's nod before continuing.* "Well… that's what we're

144

watching now. The latest batch of bots are designed to seek the cell level receptors of the nerve fibers, the locations where they can latch onto the nerve at the cellular level and fuse with it, becoming indistinguishable in any meaningful way from the nerve itself."

"You mean that once the nanobots … how did you say it… fuse with the nerve cells, there's no way to distinguish them from the nerve itself?"

Ted nods in agreement. "Well… if you had the right equipment and lots of time, you might be able to suss out the nanobots. But for the most part, once the nanobots have fused with the nerves, they're virtually undetectable. … What you're watching here is that process happening in a limited controlled environment. Once the bots are introduced, they… search…yes, that's probably the best way to describe it. They search for the appropriate receptor to bind to. Once they bind to the receptor, they integrate themselves into the cell structure itself operating as part of the cell and able to receive and transmit instructions. In a sense, they become part of the nervous system in a very real way serving to augment it and allowing specific, guided instructions to be passed to the body."

Ted and the Senator pause for a moment, watching the monitor as the nanobots in the culture move towards nerve cells, quickly attach themselves, and then merge with the cell structures.

"That's… That's remarkable…" *The Senator straightens up and faces Ted.* "Have you managed to accomplish anything like this outside of the lab? I mean beyond nanobots in a petri dish?"

"Ah… Actually Senator, we have. After we accomplished the proof of concept on a small scale as you see here, we moved on to animal studies…"

"Wait. You've tested these nanobot things in living animals? Isn't that unethical?"

"Yes, to your first question and no to the second. The next step for many medical developments often centers on animal research. However, we only used injured animals in our work. Our objective was to see how effective the bots would be in assimilating themselves into the animals' nervous systems and serving as a pathway for us to effectively manage or eliminate the animals' pain."

"I see. How did it go?"

"Quite well. After some initial failures where the bots didn't manage to latch onto the nerve cell receptors in the test animals, we discovered a minor error in the bots programming that seemed to be the problem. Once we corrected that, the bots seamlessly integrated themselves with the animals' nerve cells and the real work could begin."

"So simply managing to get the nanobots to integrate with the nervous system was just the start?"

"Exactly. Although most might rest on their laurels after achieving this sort of breakthrough, we knew that it was just the beginning of what might be possible. There were any number of avenues to go down and potential applications to be pursued."

"Such as?"

"Well… blocking pain signals for one. If we could stimulate the nervous system in a way that would block or ignore what it would normally recognize as pain, we could improve quality of life and allow the animals to do things their injuries had prevented them from doing.

Of course, it wasn't quite that simple. There was a lot of trial and error, stimulating specific nerves to determine reactions. It took quite some time, even aided by computer driven artificial intelligence, or AI, to complete an entire map of the nervous system down to the cellular level and document exactly what each level of stimulation to each individual nerve cell and cell groupings did. But once we accomplished that, the rest followed as a more or less logical extension of that work. … Would you like to see a demonstration?"

"I admit that you've gotten me intrigued. Please, if you don't mind. ."

"Not at all Senator." *Ted leans over the workstation keyboard and types. The display of the petri dish experiment disappears, to be replaced a moment later by a video with dates and times running along the bottom.* "We started small, although that's perhaps too much of a simplification because the nervous system of any animal, such as this rat, is still incredibly complex. However, using the same process I outlined a moment ago, we mapped the nervous system and successfully introduced the bots into the rat.

The first video you see here is of the rat before we attempted to use the bots to stimulate portions of the rat's nervous system. As you can see, the poor creature suffered from severe arthritis that made it painful for it to walk." *The video ran for several minutes showing the rat struggling to move from one side of a spacious enclosure to the other to try to eat food that had been placed there.* "I won't claim that we achieved success overnight, but as we improved our understanding of using the bots to stimulate specific groupings and even individual nerve cells, we did manage to improve the rat's mobility by substantially reducing its pain." *Ted pushes a button on the laptop and the monitor switches to a new video with a later date and time displayed.* "As you can see, the rat's ability to move is significantly increased." *The rat can been see moving much more quickly from one side of the enclosure to the other and even standing upright against the enclosure's side as it tries to bite a piece of cheese hanging from a hook.*

"Amazing. And that's the same rat from the first video? Did you cure its arthritis?"

"It is the same rat, Senator. We didn't cure its arthritis. I'm afraid that that would require an entirely different line of research. However, we did manage to block any pain signals the arthritis would have caused before we influenced its system through the bots."

The Senator looks away from the monitor and more directly at Ted. "Impressive. Truly impressive Ted. But I hope you've got more to show me than just a rat moving around an enclosure. I don't see how even this level of success could justify the budget you've got and the expenditures that the subcommittee has caught wind of."

Ted smiles and again hits a few keys on the keyboard. The display on the monitor changes to a new video showing another rat, in a smaller enclosure with a metal rod holding cheese on two prongs that extend out from the rod. "Ah, but we've gone beyond that Senator. We've learned how to block pain entirely. Watch." *Ted pushes a key on the keyboard and the video starts. The rat sits motionless and then walks over to the rod and sniffs at the cheese. Then, without a bit of hesitation, it stands up on its hind legs, bracing itself against the rod to grab and bite a chunk out of the cheese on one of the prongs.*

"What am I looking at here Ted? Surely there's more to this video than a rat eating some cheese…"

Ted smiles again. more broadly this time. "There is Senator. The rod has a low-level current of electricity running through it, not enough to harm the rat, but enough, under normal circumstances, to discourage it from going after the cheese"

"So you managed to increase the rat's tolerance for the charge?"

"We managed to completely block the rat's ability to even feel the charge. Imagine what that could mean, the applications in everyday life. We could reduce or eliminate anesthesia for most operations. We could improve the quality of life for people with debilitating diseases…"

"You could create super soldiers, able to fight long after most would be rendered ineffective from injuries or wounds…"

"Well, yes, I suppose we could."

"But this still looks like some scientific pipedream Ted. Unless you've got something else to show me…"

Ted looks a bit uncomfortable for a minute as though trying to decide on something. "Well, there is more. … Your clearance documents indicate that you have Beta clearance?"

The Senator raises his eyebrows, obviously intrigued by where this might be heading. "That's correct. Is there more to this facility than meets the eye? Something more that I should know beyond these parlor tricks with animals?"

Ted seems to hesitate for a moment before responding. "Yes, there is Senator. But I can't say anything more in this area. If you'd like, we could go to a more secure area where I can provide you with more details? ..."

"I'd like that very much Ted. Let's go see what you've really achieved with all that money we've spent on this place. ... Lead on."

Ted takes a moment to turn off the video on the monitor and then turn off the workstation. Then gesturing with one hand towards a thick, reinforced door at the other end of the lab, he leads the Senator across the room. After swiping his badge through a reader by the door, Ted types in a sequence of numbers on a keypad attached to the reader. A loud buzz is heard as the door unlocks. He pushes it and holds it open, waving for the Senator to enter. "Right this way, Senator." *They both enter and the door closes behind them.*

Grieco

□

Ted leads the Senator down a short hallway past several closed windowless doors. At the fourth door, Ted stops and turns to the Senator.

"I think you'll find this very interesting Senator. We've moved on from animal testing to actually being able to test how the biotech we've developed works, in specific cases, in humans."

"Human testing! No one's informed the Committee of this. The budget doesn't show…"

Ted holds up both hands in a placating gesture to stop the Senator. "I understand that this may come as a surprise Senator. We are scheduled to brief the Sub-Committee on this next stage of our program during our next session with you on… the 14th, I believe?"

The Senator looks somewhat mollified by Ted's statement and looks towards the door with a concerned but anticipatory look.

"Well, I'm glad to hear that, Ted. Even with classified programs, perhaps especially with them, it's essential that we be kept in the loop on developments. … I suppose you can't stop work just because you haven't briefed us on your efforts yet but still…"

"I understand completely Senator. Rest assured that we're not trying to hide anything from you. It's just that committee scheduling doesn't always keep up with the rate of successes we might be experiencing here."

"Well, Ok then. ... So what do you want to show me in this particular room?"

Ted puts one hand on the doorknob and smiles at the Senator before opening the door and motioning for him to enter. "That Senator, will be perhaps easier to explain once we go inside. Shall we?"

The Senator enters the room and Ted follows, closing the door behind them. Inside, is a smallish area marked, at the opposite side from the door, by a window providing a view into another room. In that room, what appears to be a medical technician is working with a seated man of about thirty years of age whose left leg is gone from just above the knee. The tech is examining what appears to be some sort of mechanical prosthesis and explaining something to the man. Then, the tech takes the prosthesis, bends down, and works with the man to attach it to his left leg.

"So, Ted, what exactly are we looking at here? I presume you didn't bring me in here to watch a prosthesis fitting?"

Ted smiles. "Ah ... no Senator. It is a little bit more than just that. ... Remember the work I described earlier with the nanobots and how they fuse with the nerve cells to create an interface within the body?"

"Yes, I do. But I don't see how that applies here." *Gestures towards the window.*

"Yes. I admit that it isn't readily apparent how that might apply here. But what we can't see is that the patient has already been prepped with an infusion of nanobots that have successfully fused with his nerve cells". ... *Ted lets that sink in for just a second or two.* "The prosthesis that the tech is now adjusting on the patient's leg has been designed to interface directly with the nerve endings, and the bots fused with them, in the remaining portion of the man's left leg. It takes a minute or so for the nerves to link up and integrate with the prosthesis. After that, the patient should be able to "feel" the prosthesis as though it was his original leg and gain full functionality within a few minutes. Of course, there will be a relatively short time that is required for him to "relearn" walking with the prosthesis. But even that should only take a week or so before he's able to do everything that he could before he lost his leg."

The Senator stands in silence for a few moments, watching the scene in the other room. The tech finishes adjusting the prosthesis. The tech then pushes a button on the side of the prosthesis and closes a flap that merges seamlessly with the rest of the unit. A startled look crosses the face of the patient followed by a broad grin as he slowly begins to move the artificial limb, bending it at the knee several times before attempting to stand. He almost falls at his first try but is caught by the tech who supports him until he gains his balance. Then, with a determined and focused look on his face, the patient begins to walk, tentatively but successfully, around the room. After once around the room, he sits again and begins to talk with the tech. Seeing this, Ted pushes a switch mounted on the wall near the window and it turns opaque, blocking any further view of the scene.

"As you can see Senator, we've achieved a degree of success with our program that no one else has even managed to get close to. It has the potential to revolutionize the treatment of accident victims, amputees, the neurologically impaired, and help those with Multiple Sclerosis, Muscular Dystrophy, and even Amyotrophic Lateral Sclerosis. There might even be some applications for Alzheimer's and other forms of dementia."

Little Book of Stories

The Senator stands thoughtfully for a moment gazing at the now opaqued window, then turns back to Ted, "I see. … What you've achieved here is truly remarkable. I've never seen anything like it. In fact, I doubt if anyone anywhere has even begun to approach the basics of what you've done." *He pauses, as though searching for the right words, before continuing.* "If this works as you say it does, and as your demonstration indicates it does, … then this will indeed revolutionize medical treatment for the types of conditions you mentioned. … I do have a question though."

"Ask away Senator. I'll do my best to answer any questions you might have."

"You've talked about the nanobots fusing with the nerve cells, thus allowing an interface to be established through which stimulation can be provided to control bodily functions, enhance them, and even replace them as in the case of a missing limb. Have I described it correctly?"

"Fundamentally, the way you've described it is correct. And your question Senator?"

"Yes. Well, how are you able to access the nanobots once they've fused with the nerve cells in order to get them to do what you want them to do?"

"Ah… That is a very good question. I'll try to explain it as much as I can without going into too much technical jargon or getting down in the weeds."

"I'd appreciate that. I've got a pretty good grasp of technology and science on a basic level. However, I have to admit that when folks start getting into the deep end with language jammed full of jargon, equations, and tech specs,

I might get the gist of it but the real detailed stuff is wasted on me."

Ted smiles. "I'll try and keep it simple Senator". *He thinks for a moment.* "Perhaps it's easiest just to say that we've developed a proprietary communication system that allows us to remotely access and provide commands to the fused nanobots."

"So, you don't need to directly interface with them with some sort of device embedded in the body?"

"No, we don't. Now it is true that in some cases, like the prosthesis you saw, some devices are designed with an inherent capability to communicate directly, interface if you will, with nanobots fused with the nerves. However, in general, we can provide directions and updates to the bots from a device much like this one." *Ted reaches into a pocket and pulls out a small handheld device with a flat touchscreen.*

"That looks very much like a smartphone."

"Yes, it does, doesn't it? We wanted to have something small, like a cellphone, so, we reversed engineered from one and kept the computing power and communication packages, although we did change the transmitter. Then we piggybacked on the basic package and added the functionalities we needed to communicate with the bots."

"Clever. And that device can control the nanobots inside the body?"

"Yes, it can. Although, as I've said, devices like the prosthesis have a built-in ability to interface directly with the bots."

Little Book of Stories

"What's the range of a device like that?"

Ted looks down at the device in his hand. "Ah… this device has a fairly limited range. A couple of hundred feet at best. But if we were to link into commercially available cellphone technology, I suppose we could remotely communicate with nanobots anywhere there was a cell signal available. … Why do you ask?"

"Oh, nothing really. Just a vague idea starting to form in the back of my head. … I do have another question if you don't mind?"

"Certainly Senator. Please go ahead."

"Are you able to target the nanobots to just limited parts of the body … to treat specific conditions?"

Ted looks thoughtful. "We tried doing that in the early stages of our research once we'd managed to perfect the nanobots, their fusion capability, and the interface. However, we discovered that if we inserted only a small number of bots into a specific area, they would indeed fuse with nerve cells at that location. But that didn't prove to be effective. The bots had a tendency to… wander away from the desired location and become so diffuse that we couldn't manage to get them to do what we wanted to them to do."

"I see. … How did you manage to overcome that problem?"

"We went back to the drawing board so to speak. We returned to the maps of the nervous system we'd created and used them to determine which areas the bots had migrated to. We added a transponder to the bots so we could trace their movement in the body and determine just where they had fused with nerve cells."

Ted fiddles with the device in his hand for a moment and one of the walls of the room lights up with a wide display showing a comprehensive map of the human nervous system. "This has been much simplified for demonstration purposes, but I think you'll get the idea. The red markers show nerve cells without the presence of nanobots. This slide shows the before state, with no bots introduced."

Ted does something on the handheld device and the display changes. Green dots begin to appear in various parts of the nervous system map, changing to blue as they overlap with the red markers. "As bots are infused into the body, they migrate throughout the body, finding and fusing with nerve cells they encounter. We discovered that even a few non-fused nerve cells could inhibit the ability to stimulate the nerves, even at a different location, to do what we were attempting to do. So, we overcompensated by essentially dumping millions of bots into the body, until all the red markers turned blue. Any extra bots left over continued to circulate in the body, replacing faulty bots or fusing with newly formed nerve cells as they grew. The presence of extra bots in the body did no discernable harm to the subjects and served as a safety system of sorts. A repair service, if you will, for fused bots that were no longer functioning correctly. Maybe the best way to describe it is like an interlinked network that self-corrects when it detects a problem."

"So once the nanobots are established, the network monitors and self-corrects any problems it might detect. And the nanobots fuse with every nerve cell all across the body?"

"Yes, exactly."

The Senator frowns, contemplating all that he'd been told that day. "Ted, let me congratulate you on the work you've done here. It's revolutionary, disruptive. It has the potential to change everything across multiple disciplines in medicine, science, ... and other areas. But I'm going to recommend that your budget be cut."

A look of startled surprise and dismay crosses Ted's face. "But why Senator? I don't understand. ... We've made astonishing progress in our work..."

"Yes, you have Ted. And I sympathize with your desire to do more. Really, I do. But it seems that your work has progressed to the point where it should be turned over to the medical side of the house. I'm going to recommend that your work be transferred to DoD's medical research team so they can take full advantage of the advances you've made in prostheses and the potential to alleviate the other conditions you've talked about today."

The Senator pauses, looking Ted directly in the eyes. "And frankly Ted, I'm concerned about the potential for abuse your research presents. If these nanobots could be contained within only one portion of the body, to accomplish a specific medical procedure, then that would be one thing. But to have nanobots fused with every nerve cell at every part of the human body just seems to be begging for someone to do mischief, ... to do harm as much as they could do good." *He continues to look directly at Ted.* "Why, I suppose that if you can command a part of the body to do something, you can also command those nerve cells to turn something off. This technology you've developed could kill just as easily as it could heal."

"I assure you Senator, we would never do something like that…"

"And I believe you Ted. But once the genie is out of the bottle, I can't be sure that someone else won't use it for less benign purposes. … I'll still want you engaged with the medical folks, to design failsafes to ensure that these nanobots can't be used for nefarious purposes. … You've done great work Ted, but I just can't let it continue."

Ted looks dismayed and disappointed, "I have to say that I don't agree with you Senator. We've instituted enough safeguards in the program to prevent it being misused by someone else. But I can understand your concerns."

"Again. I'm sorry Ted, but it has to be this way. … Now if the tour is over, I need to get back to the office."

Still looking disappointed, Ted nods in understanding. "I suppose you have a meeting you need to get to…"

"No, no. I set aside the entire day for this visit. I just have a ton of paperwork waiting for me what with markups of the new budget bill and prepping for next week's townhall."

Ted brightens somewhat. "Well… if you do have a little more time, I do have one more thing to show you that I think you'll find instructive as you consider how to manage our budget."

"More than what you've already shown me?"

Ted smiles, if a bit sadly. "Well, yes. I was saving it for last in hopes that it might improve our chances for a bump up in next year's budget." *Ted holds up his hands as the Senator opens his mouth to speak.* "I know you've already made up your mind on transferring our work to the medical folks, but I think you'll still want to see this."

The Senator smiles back at Ted. "Thank you for understanding. It's never easy to hear this sort of news, especially when the program is your baby and you've put your blood and sweat into making it a reality. ... I should get back, but I admit that you've got me more than a little intrigued with whatever you're teasing here. ... I guess another" ... *Looks at Ted quizzically* ... "hour won't matter. I can always do some reading before bed tonight. ... So, what have you got for me now?"

Ted noticeably brightens. "Again Senator, it's much easier to show you than to try and tell you. ... If you'd be so kind as to come his way..."

Ted walks to the door to the hallway and opens it ushering the Senator though it into the hall. Ted then turns left and leads him past several doors. Finally, they reach a heavy door at the end of the hall with a keypad next to the handle. Ted keys in a series of numbers and is rewarded with a loud click. With some effort, he pulls the door open and holds it as the Senator enters. Ted follows, allowing the door to close behind him with a thud that echoes dully in the space beyond.

Grieco

□

Ted and the Senator are in a space that looks like a small anteroom. There are three closed doors on the opposite side of the space. Ted leads the Senator to the middle door, opens it, and gestures for the Senator to enter. Once he does, Ted follows, closing the door behind him. Two comfortable looking office chairs sit in the center of a mid-sized room. Ted motions for the Senator to take one of them. After the Senator settles into it, Ted takes the other. Two large, opaqued windows fill the walls on either side of the room. Once Ted is seated, the Senator looks over at him.

"Where did you find these chairs Ted? I have to say that this is the most comfortable one I've ever sat in. I wouldn't mind having one of these in my office. Most chairs, even the most expensive ones, are either so plush that you sink into them or are so hard that you can't stand sitting for more than a few minutes at a time. But this one...," *He rocks in the chair just a bit as if trying to get even more comfortable,* "this one I think I could sit in for hours. It just seems to actively adjust to me as I move." *The Senator shifts position several times as if trying to see if he can find a position that is uncomfortable.* "Huh... I want one of these. You'll have to give the name of the manufacturer."

Ted smiles, evidently more at ease now. "I'm glad you like it. These are from a small manufacturer we found locally. Real magicians with chairs. We find that folks are more at ease if they have something comfortable to sit in. I'll have my staff get you the info after we finish our session."

"So, Ted, what have you got to show me." *The Senator gestures at the windows.* "From the looks of it, I'd say you've got something behind one of those windows that you think will impress the hell out of me."

Ted laughs at this and responds. "Well, I certainly think that you will never see the world in quite the same way after we're done here today." *He pauses for a few seconds, then stands up and moves to one of the windows. Taking the handheld device out of his pocket, he turns to the Senator.* "You remember our discussion earlier about how the nanobots migrate throughout the body to fuse with all the individual nerve cells?"

"Sure. You had to overdo the dosing of nanobots in order to ensure that the interface for specific functions could be reliable, that you could send the appropriate stimuli to the right nerves to correct or improve a particular medical condition."

Ted nods. "That's right and it's a pretty good summary of what we've shown you thus far. However, over time and a great deal of trial and error, we discovered that having those bots everywhere throughout the body gave us the capability to do much more than just that."

"More than just controlling prostheses and regulating body functions…"

"Correct. … Once we had managed to successfully get the bots to fuse with nerve cells and interface with the nervous system, it opened up a gateway for a variety of stimuli that could be used to influence various organs, muscles, and the entire body."

"Sure. I can understand how that might be possible. What else did these bots allow you to do?"

"Virtually anything really. We could bypass severed spinal cords and restore function to those with paralysis. We could restore sight to those whose optic nerves were damaged. And ... quite by accident mind you ... we discovered that we could induce pain or pleasure."

The Senator appears startled by this last statement. He leans forward in his chair. "Look Ted, you had me up until that last part. You showed me the ability to interface seamlessly with prostheses. And it isn't much of a leap to see that those nanobots could serve to repair damaged nerves and restore connections, but pain and pleasure. ... I'm not sure I buy that."

Ted nods his head in understanding. "I know what you mean. We didn't realize what we'd discovered at first ourselves. It took a while before we associated stimulation of certain neural pathways with the sensations of pain or pleasure. But as we went along, we started to see repeated instances where certain signals sent to certain bots gave us repeatable instances of those sensations. We were trying to expand our knowledge of how to block pain. In doing so we discovered that by reversing the polarity of the signal sent to the bots, it had quite the oppose result."

Ted points the handheld device at the window he's standing near and pushes something on it. The window clears, revealing a room similar in size to the one he and the Senator are in. There are two chairs in the other room, much like the one the Senator is seated in. Those chairs are separated from each other by a few feet. A woman in a lab coat sits in one while a woman in street clothes sits in the other. That woman is perched on the edge of her chair gazing apprehensively at the lab-coated woman. Ted moves slightly to what looks to be an intercom panel set in the wall and pushes a button. "Ms. Jenkins, are we ready for the demonstration?"

The woman in the lab coat nods. "Yes sir. We can begin whenever you're ready."

"Thank you. Let's start, shall we? Begin at the lowest setting and increase the stimuli gradually until it's at level 6. That should suffice for an adequate demonstration. We'll leave the intercom open for now."

Ms. Jenkins nods again, stands, and reaches into a pocket in her lab coat. She pulls out a handheld device remarkably similar to the one Ted has been using throughout the tour. She swipes at the screen a couple of times and then presses her finger onto the screen and holds it, very slowly moving her finger in a circular motion. "Starting now sir."

"Thank you, Ms. Jenkins. We'll monitor things from here." *Ted turns to the Senator.* "I know it looks like nothing is happening Senator, but the subject is beginning to experience a slow warmth throughout her body as the stimulus received through the nanobots begins to take effect. As the degree of stimulus is increased, the sensation will begin to become quite unpleasant."

At this point, the seated woman begins to shift uncomfortably in her chair and begins to rub at her arms as though trying to brush away something crawling on them. "At some point, the sensation will move from being simply unpleasant to being painful."

The seated woman begins to writhe in her chair and begins to utter low moans and can be heard pleading, "No. Don't. Please stop. Please...."

Grieco

Watching the Senator's reaction, Ted continues. "Eventually, the pain simply becomes too much for a person to stand."

The seated woman falls to the floor, her body wracked in pain, jerking as her muscles react to the stimulus delivered via the nanobots. Without warning, she starts to scream, loudly, incessantly, only stopping to gasp for breath before screaming again. Ted looks over at the Senator who is staring aghast at the scene before him. "That will be enough for now Ms. Jenkins. Thank you."

Ms. Jenkins nods and gradually moves her finger in the opposite direction on the device's screen. The other woman's screams slowly lessen, then stop, and she falls into unconsciousness as the pain finally ends.

"The beauty, Senator, is that this is completely repeatable. Once the bots are in someone's system, we have complete control over them and what stimuli can be introduced."

The Senator sits, his face pale with the impact of what he's just witnessed. "Why that's monstrous…"

Ted holds up his hand to stop the Senator before he has the chance to say anything further. "Yes Senator, I completely understand. It can be quite a shock to see this sort of thing. But I do have one more demonstration for you."

Ted walks over to the other window, pushes a button on his device and the window also becomes clear. The Senator turns his chair to look at the scene within, caught up in a morbid fascination by what he's witnessed and what he might yet see. Through the window, another room, identical to the first, can be seen. As before, there are two chairs, this time with two men sitting in them, one in a lab coat, the other in street clothes. Ted moves to an intercom panel on the wall by this window and pushes a button. "Mr. Barnes, are we ready?"

The lab coated man nods his head. "Yes sir. All set here."

Ted looks at the Senator. "I think you'll find this very interesting Senator." *He turns back towards the window.* "Very well Mr. Barnes, let's proceed. Start with the system warm-up and then gradual raise it up to…" *He pauses for a moment.* "What level have you reached thus far with this subject?"

The lab coated man replies. "Level three sir."

Ted frowns for just a moment. "Hmmm. I had hoped that we would have progressed further. Still, I suppose it will have to do for purposes of a demonstration. Alright Mr. Barnes, level three it is, but use your discretion if you think level four is appropriate, at this time, for the subject."

The lab coated man nods, then reaches into his coat pocket and takes out a handheld device which he activates. Then with a circular motion, he slowly moves his hand on the device's screen.

Ted turns back to the Senator who can't seem to tear his gaze away from what is going on in the other room. "As before, even though it looks like nothing is happening, our subject is beginning to experience a slow spreading warmth as the nanobots react to the signal being transmitted to them."

Inside the other room, the man in street clothes becomes more alert, sitting up as if in anticipation of what was to come next. An almost hungry look crosses his face as the sensations stemming from the nanobots' stimuli become more pronounced. His face takes on a look of bliss and he smiles, relaxing back into the chair. His body begins to move in small jerky movements as he begins to moan and gasp in what could only be described as small fits of complete delight and pleasure.

Watching this, Ted turns to the Senator. "Right now, our subject is experiencing increasing waves of sheer pleasure flowing through every part of his body. Even if he somehow wanted to avoid it, he could not. He is held in thrall by his body's reaction to the bots' stimuli. ... I understand that it's quite addictive. Possibly a thousand times more so than crack cocaine or even fentanyl." *He turns and speaks into the intercom once again.* "What level is that Mr. Barnes?"

"3.5, sir."

"Good. Very good. ... That will do for now. Bring him down slowly, Mr. Barnes. Let's not trigger withdrawal."

"Yes sir." *The lab coated man reverses his hand motion on his device's screen, slowly reducing the nanobot stimuli to the subject. As the stimuli is lessened,* "Level 3. Level 2. Level 1." *the posture and expression of the man changes. His eyes open and his face takes on a haunted look as the intense feeling ebbs away from him. He motions desperately towards the lab coated man.* "Please... don't... don't stop...". *As the last of the sensations leave his body, he crumples into a ball, grabbing his knees with both hands and, sobbing, slowly rocks in his chair.* "Bring it back. Please, bring it back. I'll do anything. ... Anything..." *His voice fades to a whisper.*

Little Book of Stories

Ted pushes a button on his device and both windows become opaque. He turns towards the Senator whose face shows a mix of horror and fascination. "So, you see Senator, our work here has applications far beyond what we've reported thus far."

Ted's face takes on an enthusiastic look as he leans into his pitch. "Just think about it. This technology would be priceless when dealing with prisoners, terrorists, criminals. … Interrogations would leave no marks. No sign that a suspect had ever been in custody. They would be literally unable to resist the stimuli provided by the bots and we could continue those stimuli indefinitely, whether a subject was in custody or not. The potential for intelligence gathering, for behavioral modification, for turning enemy agents, diplomats, and others into actively working for us … is limitless."

The Senator, still visibly shocked by what he has just witnessed, makes an effort to gather himself before responding. "I can see why some might see this… thing that you've created as a good thing for medicine and even science, but… this… this could easily be misused, … abused if it got into the wrong hands. Frankly, I don't understand how you could have gotten anyone to volunteer to undergo this kind of torture and… whatever that last thing you showed me was."

Ted smiles, a small secretive smile that made the Senator shiver, just a bit, inside. "Pleasure, Senator. Pure, unadulterated pleasure. Subject a person to enough of that stimulus for long enough and they will do anything for you… anything to keep it and to get it back when you take it away. Pain, … that stimulus is excellent for interrogations, to break down a person's ability to resist, … to quite simply, break them. But pleasure, given on a regular basis, with the ability to withhold it at any time, will make a person serve whoever holds the key to that pleasure." *Ted paused, looking from one opaqued window to the other.* "And Senator, the subjects, that you just saw, weren't volunteers."

The Senator sinks back into his chair, staring at Ted with horror. "Not volunteers… That's completely unethical. How could you…"

Ted holds up both hands in a placating gesture, cutting off anything else the Senator might say. "Relax Senator. These people don't exist."

"Don't exist. I just saw them. One was screaming in pain while the other was… whatever that was."

Ted nods, a sympathetic look on his face. "Perhaps I should have said that the subjects were invisible people. Homeless. On the edge of existence with no one to know if they lived or died. Hundreds of them simply disappear every year with society paying no attention to that at all. We simply scooped a few off the streets, fed them, took care of their medical needs, and then made them subjects in some of our more… extensive tests of the technology."

The Senator leans forward in his chair, anger now overtaking his other feelings about what he's just seen. "You might think that's laudable Ted, but it isn't. I'm not going to support giving you one more cent to continue this, … this monstrosity of an experiment. Even with the medical care you've provide to those people, it's still a violation of their rights and completely unethical to boot. Never mind injecting them with nanobots that you then use to subject them to these … experiments."

Little Book of Stories

Ted's face takes on a disappointed look. "I'm sorry to hear that, Senator. I had hoped that we could count on your support ...convince you that our work is worthwhile." *He pauses for a moment, a thoughtful expression forming creases on his forehead* "1 do wonder though..."

"What? What do you wonder?"

"What made you think that we injected the subjects with the nanobots?"

The Senator freezes, still outraged but caught completely off-guard by the question. "Well... from everything you said about the nature of your... experiments, it's only logical that you had to use injection or some kind of infusion to get the nanobots into the bodies of these poor unfortunates."

Ted smiles at this, nodding again as he replied. "Yes, well, I can see why you might assume that to be the case. And we did do that, in the beginning. But the nanobots are so tiny, so infinitesimal in size, that millions would fit in a teaspoon of water. Why trillions upon trillions of them could be introduced into a glass of water and the person drinking it would be none the wiser. ... That's how we introduced the nanobots into our subjects. They may still not realize what we've done to them. All they know is that we have the power to cause them pain or pleasure at a touch of the screen of a device, ... just like this one."

Ted shows the Senator the device he's been using throughout the tour. "Why even a cup of coffee would do just fine as a method of introducing nanobots into a person's body."

Grieco

The Senator stiffens, his face taking on an expression of horrified comprehension.

Ted nods again, his smile growing broader. "I know. I know. It's discomforting to think that something as simple as a cup of coffee could put one at such a... disadvantage."

Holding the device in one hand, Ted places his index finger on it and begins a slow rotating motion on the screen. "That warm sensation you feel throughout every fiber of your body is the nanobots interfacing with your nervous system." *He stops the motion of his finger on the device's screen.* "Are you certain you won't change your mind on our funding? ... No? ... That's quite... unfortunate." *He resumes moving his finger on the device's screen.* "What a shame. Believe me, ... I sincerely regret that it's come to this."

Ted smiles again, a slow sad smile, before continuing. "Now, what will it be Senator, pleasure... or pain?"

Winter Tales

Christmas Angst

The park was dressed in its winter best, white frosting the empty trees and ground alike, disguising the dirt and grime of city life. A magical place, it was somewhere to escape from the cares of everyday life without having to travel very far or try very hard to do so. It was a haven of sorts for my daughter and me, a place where nothing else mattered but the playground area and the peaceful time spent together there. In my case, that mostly meant watching my daughter play with the other kids brought by other parents seeking the same escape and refuge from the world without.

So there we were, us parents, sitting on the park benches watching our kids play. Most of us anyway. The woman to my left seemed more interested in a book she'd pulled from a tote bag situated at her feet. Most of the kids, hers included I assumed, were over by the teeter totter, waiting their turn to leave the slightly frozen ground for a few moments as their backsides bounced at the top of the long plank's rise towards the sky. I had only glanced away for a moment or so but when I turned back, I saw my daughter stamp her feet and gesture at a little boy. Obviously upset about something, she turned and headed my way.

She ran up to me, her mouth set in a downward pout with a cross look on her face that spoke volumes of the temper she might yet prove to have.

"Daddy. Matt says there's no such thing as Santa Claus. I called him a liar. He is one, isn't he? Santa Claus is real. I just know he is."

She buried herself against my winter coat and held on to me for all she was worth. Looking down at the top of my daughter's head, I couldn't help but wonder how we had gotten to this particular crisis so quickly. She was only five after all. This existential kind of stuff wasn't supposed to happen for several more years yet. I shook my head in silent bemusement and regret that it had come this soon.

She must have felt my movement for she pulled back some and looked up. Her brown eyes were full of trust and confidence that I would set her straight on this terribly important subject. "Well?" She asked. "He is real, isn't he?"

I gazed down at her and stroked her chestnut hair while I tried desperately to come up with an answer that wouldn't shatter her long held beliefs about the red suited fellow with the belly laugh and magic sleigh and reindeer. It was only a few seconds or so, but it seemed like forever as a thousand possible replies flew through my head like snowflakes in a gusty wind, soaring here and there but never seeming to quite come to rest anyplace at all. Finally, I said the only thing I could.

"Do you want to believe in Santa Claus?"

She looked at me for a moment in surprise. Then her brow furrowed and her eyes became unfocused as she looked at something I clearly couldn't see. She tended to do that whenever she thought about something particularly hard and this question was obviously worthy of her deepest attention. After a time she nodded her head, eyes seeing me and the world again and brow becoming smooth and flat with her decision.

"Yes." Was all she said although she continued to look at me as though waiting for something more.

I had nothing. I'd stopped believing in Santa by the time I was ten and steeped in the realities of a hard, cruel world I had long ago banished thoughts of Christmas miracles and talking snowmen to that place where all childhood dreams and hopes are locked away. But she was too young for that. I didn't want reality for her. Not now. Not yet.

Yeah, I had nothing. So I asked a different question, gently hoping she might help me find a way to preserve this slice of innocence a little longer.

"Why Amy? Can you tell me why you want Santa to be real?"

She thought about it for just a second or two before she nodded and firmly replied. "Because it's better that way."

It was my turn to be surprised and without much thought I heard myself give back "What... What do you mean by that?"

She only smiled at me and hugged me tight again before dancing back a step with her reply. "Silly daddy. Because it is. Everyone knows that."

"We do?"

Her head nodded twice again. "Uh huh."

My turn. Still nothing. "Well ok. Everyone knows that. But why do *you* think it's better?"

She cocked her head the way she does when she thinks I've said a particularly funny thing that maybe is just common sense to her. "Oh Daddy... You know." She twirled around just a bit as though she couldn't stay rooted to one spot for very long. "EVERYONE KNOWS!"

I leaned in closer and used my best conspiratorial voice. "Well sure. But why don't you make believe I don't and tell me anyway."

She looked at me again with a hint of something I was sure I'd see again in the coming years. Exasperation maybe? I just smiled my best smile to show I was truly interested in what she had to say.

"Well…" she began. "Santa is the bestest person in the whole world. He doesn't care if you're big or small, have lots of money or none at all, where you live, or any of that stuff. He only cares about you and what you do. Like the music says. *(singing)* He sees you when you're sleeping. He knows when you're awake. He knows if you've been bad or good. So be good for goodness sake."

I couldn't help but laugh just a little at the sight of her standing there, head back, eyes bright with joy and anticipation as she sang those old words. "So it's important to be good?"

She stopped for a second and looked at me again. "Why sure daddy. Everyone should be good." She paused for a second, her eyes losing focus for just a second. "Course nobody can be good all the time. But Santa knows that too. That's why Bobby still gets presents every year even though he's mean to me at school sometimes."

"Bobby is mean to you?"

"Uh huh." She nodded to me with an earnestness that only a five-year-old could have. "He takes my crayons when we're coloring and always cuts in line and… and other stuff that I don't like."

I smiled inwardly and thought that if this was the worst thing she experienced in her life then she would be truly blessed. "But if Bobby's mean to you, why would Santa still give him presents?"

She got a serious look on her face for just a moment as though what she was about to say was terribly important and that I should give it the attention it deserved. So I did, leaning forward from the park bench to focus only on her.

Grieco

"Well..." she said. "Santa sees everything. Even what's inside... 'n everybody's got some good inside. Don't they Daddy?"

My turn again. I paused for a second, summoning up what I hoped were the right words. "Ah, uh sure, sure they do." Even to me it sounded less than affirming.

She didn't seem to notice though. "Even bad people?"

"Ah... yeah. Even bad people have some good inside them."

She nodded solemnly and spoke as if to herself. "Well that 'splains it then."

This puzzled me. "Explains what exactly?"

She looked at me, her eyes full of knowledge and hope. "The coal of course."

"The coal?"

"Uh huh. Bad people get a lump of coal from Santa."

Relieved that it was something as simple as this I sat back a bit. "Of course. The lump of coal."

She grabbed my hand and pulled it just a bit, the way she did when she thought I wasn't paying attention to something she was trying to say. "No Daddy it's not that way."

"Not what way?"

"You know... that Santa gives them some coal as a punishment because they're bad."

Now I was even more puzzled. "He doesn't? Then why does he give them the coal?"

She looked at me with wisdom far beyond her years and leaned in as though confiding a secret to me. "It's a present too."

"A present?"

She nodded twice to emphasize her words. "Uh huh. Santa wants them to know that they've been bad but also wants them to know that they haven't been forgotten."

"Oh." was all I could muster.

She nodded again, more vigorously this time. "He sees the good in them and the coal is a kinda promise. That if they can be just a little more good next year, he'll bring them something better. Santa wants people to be good and his presents, even the coal, are a promise that he'll always be there watching and ready to show he cares at Christmas time."

I thought that maybe I finally understood. "So Santa helps people be better than they might otherwise be because of his Christmas promise."

She nodded again, her eyes full of excitement that I finally got it. "And that's why it's better that Santa is real." She danced a little bit, jiggling with the energy of childhood just aching to get back to play. "So Santa is real, isn't he Daddy?" She asked one more time, already knowing the answer in her heart.

I smiled at her and gave the only answer I could. "Yes Amy. Santa is real."

She squealed with delight at my confirmation of her belief and ran back to the teeter totter where her friends were taking turns going up and down as though the world depended on it. And perhaps it did.

Grieco

"Kind of like God isn't he?" said the women to my left all bundled up against the winter chill.

"I'm sorry but what?"

"Santa." She said. "Your daughter's views are kind of what we think of when we think of God."

My puzzlement must have shown on my face for she continued.

"We think of God as being all good and being able to know everything we do. He sees into our very hearts and knows us as we truly are. Even his punishments are a promise, that if we only try our best to be good and do good things, we will receive his gift at the end of our time. Much like the gifts at Christmas are our reward for being good the rest of the year."

She looked at me intently as expecting some sort of answer. My mind reached desperately for something that would satisfy her without drawing me into what promised to be a much longer discussion. "I suppose." Inane sounding even to me but I wasn't willing to engage in that discussion. Not now. Not here.

To my immense relief, she turned back to her book seemingly satisfied at my acknowledgment of her unsolicited observation. I paused, glancing sideways at her to make sure I was truly safe. Yep. Escaped that one. She seemed fully absorbed once again by whatever truth or fiction she held firmly in her hands. I leaned back and relaxed, letting the tension, I hadn't known was there, melt away in the warmth of my daughter's innocent wisdom.

Of course Santa's real. Everyone knows that. It's just better that way.

A Winter's Tale

The Kingdom had fallen on hard times. The people were poor, with little to eat, and the taxes were outrageously high. In the depths of the cruel, harsh winter, rebellion spread throughout the land. Battles raged, neighbor was set against neighbor and noble against common folk. Finally, the snows of December forced the rebels to huddle miserably within their sodden, drafty huts, within their barren, windswept camp, miles from the nearest village.

Their leader lived no better than his men, barely surviving from one day to the next, but maintaining a confident face to all to sustain the spirits of those he led. Still, inside, he felt despair as he looked at the conditions in which they suffered, knowing that they were near the end of their endurance.

Thus it was, in the midst of this late December despair, that a sentry brought an elderly, white-haired man of undetermined years to the hut of the rebel leader. The rebel, no stranger to kindness for all the violence he had seen, immediately offered the old man, clad all in red, the chair he had himself occupied but a moment before.

"Who are you, old man, to appear in my camp, in this weather, alone, with no provisions, victuals, or means to survive the snow?"

"Some call me Chris, but you may call me Claus." said the man, while gratefully easing himself into the proffered chair.

Smiling at the lack of offered words, the rebel ran his hand through his graying, thinning hair and asked, "Still Claus, what are you doing here?"

Grieco

With a groan that shook the loose boards of the hut, Claus shifted in his seat and, with a surprisingly sharp and knowing stare, did not respond but said, "What is it you most want?"

"What?!"

"What is it you most want?" repeated Claus.

Shaking his head at the strangeness of the question, the rebel pondered for a moment and responded, "I want peace and justice, warmth, food, and shelter for my men, and a chance to make a free life for me and mine."

Claus nodded somberly, saying, "A tall order that. As for justice, you'll have to make your own. The rest..."

The hut door was flung open, interrupting Claus, as a man, wrapped warmly against the winter wind, entered with the sound of distant cheering.

"My Lord, I have a message from the King!"

Annoyed by the intrusion, the rebel bristled, "I am no Lord man! Out with your message!"

"But you are a Lord, and higher still I warrant should the message mean as I deem it does. The old King is dead. His son has no stomach for this war and bids you make an end of it. On his part, he grants you this territory as domain and asks that you but keep the border secure against his enemies. As token of his word, he gives to you the castle Craigmoor, fully stocked and ready, as your residence but a day's ride from here. With this, he grants you the Lord's right of justice over this land and all who dwell here."

Stunned, the rebel backed across the hut and sank into the chair sitting empty by the wall. All that he had asked was in this moment given to him! With the sudden memory of the red clad man, the rebel searched the room with joyous eyes but to no avail.

And thus, in the very moment of his triumph, found himself a rebel without a Claus.

Grieco

The cops all flash their lights

The family gathered 'round the tree
to share some Christmas cheer
when suddenly just right outside
a flashing light appeared.
The youngest climbed up on a chair
to look out at the night
and asked his parents how it was
the sky was lit with lights.

The family rose as one to look
to see what youngest saw
when what to everyone's surprise
they found it was the law.
Not one, nor two, nor five, nor ten
patrol cars did they see
but all of them outside at once.
Oh how could this all be?

Then from the comfy, corner chair
where grandfather sat,
they heard him speak a certain truth
that set them all aback.
He told them in a firm, strong voice,
they shouldn't be surprised.
This happened outside every year
though never advertised.

"The cops all flash their lights at night at Christmas,
to light the way for their old buddy Nick,
so he can bring his toys
to the girls and to the boys
in this neighborhood on Christmas."

Little Book of Stories

The family stared in wonder
at this belovéd man
and didn't simply disbelieve
because of his long span
of years that brought him knowledge
of things they'd never seen
but still they stood in wonder
at just what this all could mean.

"How come I've never seen this?"
asked the father of the clan.
Grandfather just snorted,
"Did you look outside young man?
Everyone at Christmas
tends to focus here inside.
Police sirens or their lights,
they tend to take in stride.

All across the country
folks hurry to their beds
so old Saint Nick will visit them
with gifts and toys and sleds.
If they see some lights outside,
they simply close the blinds
for cops out on a Christmas eve
is the last thing on their minds.

But the cops all flash their lights at night at Christmas.
They line up in the alleys and the streets.
They help bring Christmas joy
to every girl and boy
in every neighborhood on Christmas."

And as the family looked outside
they saw a sudden flash
and heard the jingle of sleigh bells

Grieco

followed by a sudden crash
like hooves and runners on the roof
above their very heads
and all of them in haste then ran
to jump into their beds.

Their grandfather just shook his head
and softly, softly laughed
as from the family's fireplace
he felt a sudden draft.
And in the twinkling of an eye
the man in red was there
and waved him back when grandfather
offered him his chair.

Then old Saint Nick just turned
and set about his task
and when he'd finished nice and neat
gave grandfather his flask.
They toasted to the folk outside
who'd kept the sky so bright
and guided Santa and his sleigh
to all the homes that night.

For the cops all flash their lights at night at Christmas
to guide dear Santa's reindeer on their way
but once the toast was done
old Nick just quickly spun
and left the way he came that night at Christmas.

Then grandfather sat back down again
into his comfy chair
as the lights then one by one
turned off their bright, bright glare.
He knew that Nick was on his way
to do appointed tasks

Little Book of Stories

and as he sipped from Santa's flask
he simply smiled and laughed.

For he knew the cops all flash their lights at Christmas
to guide Santa through the sky upon his sleigh.
But once he's on his way,
there's no need for them to stay.
Their job is done for yet another Christmas.

Yes, the cops all flash their lights at night at Christmas
to light the way for their old buddy Nick.
They help Santa and his crew,
all night the whole world through,
to bring joy to everyone each year at Christmas.

Grieco

Two Worlds

It had snowed the past two days, the kind of wet, thick snow that coats the ground and makes the world look like something out of a painting. Shades of green combined with clumps of white as pines and conifers bent and bowed to bear the extra weight.

Everything looked perfect, the kind of scene that brought my childhood back in a rush of memories of snow and sleds and laughter flowing freely as we jumped and slid our way through the day. Even the sharp, quick wind that crept under the edges of my coat to chill my bones seemed somehow more bearable as I scraped the windshield clear of the snow and ice that had built up during the storm. Funny how a little snow can trick you into forgetting that the world is still there, hiding its flaws under that pure, thick mantle that seems to transform everything.

Two days of snow. Not much by New England standards, but still, it had played havoc with holiday preparations as snowplows worked to clear the roads and folks shoveled out just enough to let them slowly make their way to streets covered in that mix of sand and ice designed to make any trip a tad exciting. Fool that I was, I soon found myself with those stalwarts who, slipping and sliding down hills and around steep sloped curves, had journeyed out for those last few Christmas gifts and the stocking stuffers they had meant to pick up days before.

Thus it was that I found myself in the checkout line at Job Lot, precious stuffers in hand, waiting my turn in my warm farmer's coat as the girl rang up the items for the woman in front of me. Maybe it wasn't the best store, with a mix of bargain goods at bargain prices, rows stacked high with rugs, home goods, and assorted items that other stores might have passed on. There was even a pallet of portable generators over by the side wall next to the pots and pans and plaid flannel shirts, all seconds by the looks of them. No, maybe not the best of stores, but it had the advantage of being close and on a day like today, that was all the incentive I needed to forgo the forty minute drive to the quality stores of the nearest mall.

"Just because I'm poor doesn't mean I don't have money." The voice of the women in front of me pulled me from my thoughts. The cashier paused with a questioning look as she looked at the items in the woman's cart. She eyed the woman, trying not to offend, but clearly not inclined to believe that the woman could afford the assorted group of essentials, bird feed, and toys gathered in her cart. The woman was roughly dressed in clothes and jacket that showed their age. They weren't dirty, just well-worn and mended in a way that marked the care taken to make them presentable and wearable well past the time that others would have discarded them for something new.

Something in the cashier's look must have hurt for the woman said, "Look. I counted five hundred dollars in change this morning before I came here. Just ring them up. I can pay." The cashier looked at the cart, then shrugged and began to scan the items as the woman placed them in front of her.

"Can I help?" The woman turned and looked at me. I hadn't intended to get involved but somehow…

"Why would you want to do that?" the woman asked, her eyes taking on a shadowed, wary look.

"Well, it's almost Christmas and I thought…" my voice trailed off.

"You thought that you'd help the poor woman in front of you pay for her things." she shot back, and I couldn't help but hear the tone of bitterness and regret that filled her voice.

"Well yes. Ah sort of. I mean…"

The woman's eyes softened some as she watched me search for words. "Look mister. I'm not ungrateful for the offer. But I can fend for myself. There's nothing wrong with being poor. I'm no different than anyone else. Maybe I can't afford the finer things in life. And maybe I have to scrape and save just to buy a few nice things. But I work two jobs. I pay my rent. And I raise two children just fine on my own with no help from anyone." She turned to the cashier who had paused again at our exchange. "Keep ringing those things up. No need to stop."

"But can I pay for some of those things? Perhaps the toys…"

The woman looked back at me and I glimpsed a deep-seated longing that showed for just an instant on her face. She measured her words as she replied. "That's very kind of you. But those toys are gifts for my sons. They should come from me, not from some stranger, well-meaning as you are, who just happened to be behind me in the checkout line. They may not be much, but I worked hard to afford them. It wouldn't be the same. Call it pride if you will but they're my kids and I'll provide for them. Especially at Christmas."

"Well if I can't pay for them, is there something I can get for you? … Something that you want?"

The woman stopped, looking up from laying coins on the counter. She smiled, a brief, short, sad smile that gave her face beauty and grace. "I want many things mister." She looked me straight in the eyes. "Listen. You seem like a good man, but none of the things I want are things that you can buy for me. And the things I need, well…" She gestured at the bags laying on the counter. "those, … those I can pay for myself." She smiled once more then turned to gather them up. Bags in hand she turned once more, "But thank you. Your kindness means a lot to me. Merry Christmas."

"Merry Christmas." I replied as the woman moved to the store's door and to the cold beyond. I gazed after her for a moment then reached into my pocket for my credit card to pay.

"A hard case huh." the cashier said as she handed me the receipt. She smiled in a way that said without words that we two were somehow different than the woman. Better off. Maybe just better.

"Oh. I don't know…" I replied slowly. "She seemed alright to me."

The cashier smiled again, clearly not agreeing with me. "Well maybe… Merry Christmas sir. Come again soon."

"Merry Christmas." I replied and turned to make my way home. As I left, I pulled my scarf more closely round my neck and zipped my jacket to the neckline. Perhaps it was just my imagination but, somehow, the day seemed colder than before.

Christmas Gray

She seemed out of place, walking the nearly empty streets on this of all days, her cloak of deepest gray contrasting starkly with the freshly fallen snow.

She was a sad figure, all alone on a day when no one should be. Her face seemed kind but then I am no judge of character. I have seen better days and may not be one that you would choose to speak with if you walked these streets. But still she stopped, when she could have walked by.

You could tell that she was weary, within her cloak of gray, worn down by daily cares and the thousand worries of a life now in its middle years. Her smile was an echo of a brighter time and spoke of joy too seldom found in recent years.

She moved with grace and gentle ease not diminished by time, yet she wore fatigue like a leaden mantle weighing down her being 'til she seemed to stoop under the weight of it.

Riches do not make the woman more than what she is. And though her clothes spoke well of her success, the spirit, that may have marked her once, had fled and left this weary soul behind.

She did not speak. She had no need to. She merely paused, immersed in thoughtful silence and then moved on down the street. Still, though the lights were bright, and music rang with season's cheer, she took no note of it.

She paused before a window filled with memories and gazed with longing undisguised at family scene within. She made no move to brush away the single tear that marked her perfect face. The tear clung there, glistening with reflected light, lingering until it slowly fell to strike the pavement near her feet.

She shivered, as if the quickening wind had reached beneath her winter cloak to chill her very soul, and, as if rousing from a long-sought dream, slowly turned to go.

I know not of her worries. I cannot know her cares. But I know the money that she gave me will feed me tonight and for the days to come and I thank her for it.

I watched from where I sat upon a wall of bare, cold stone and wished her well as bitter wind blew and snow began to fall from shrouded skies.

She shivered once again and pulled her cloak more tightly to her as she moved away, disappearing in the swirling snow and haze, wrapped tightly for warmth, wrapped tightly for security, wrapped tightly in her solitude within her winter cloak, her long thick cloak, her cloak of Christmas gray.

Grieco

A Christmas Story

It was still early for me to be headed out. I knew that. After all, the annual Christmas Eve party at the Hospital wasn't for another couple of hours. I'd done my best to scrape up presents for the kids stuck there during the holidays, but I still felt bad. I'd only managed to get stuff from the Dollar Store… little stuff… nothing really worthy of the name gift… but still… I'd managed to get something for each of them. That was something, I guess.

So, here I was, driving through a late afternoon snowstorm, my car kicking up slush and ice, trying to get there early enough to let me get everything set up. It wouldn't be much of a Christmas for them, but at least they wouldn't be forgotten. Each and every one of them kids would have a present… all neatly wrapped… with their name on it. The bag with the gifts was on the floor behind me and my Santa suit was slung along the backseat. It really didn't fit all that well and the beard was pretty obviously fake… but the kids never seemed to mind. They were always glad that Santa had remembered them… even if he never seemed to be able to bring them much.

I gotta say that I was surprised to see him trudging along by the side of the road… right about mile marker 10, if I remember rightly. I recognized the suit immediately. It was the same as mine… red with just the right amount of white fringe along the hems and seams. His beard and hair matched the color of the fringe and, under his Santa hat, it looked like he was bone weary as he slogged along, empty bag over his shoulder, pushing his way through the stuff left over from the snowplows.

I had to stop. There was no way I was gonna let a fellow Santa be out in this weather if I could help it. I pulled over… just a little bit in front of where he was walking, rolled down my window, and waited 'til he caught up.

"Hey there old timer." I said out the window.

He stopped, made his way up to the window and leaned his heavyset frame on the door. "Hey yourself, young fellow. Can I do something for you?" came his response.

Well, I have to say that I was taken aback. Here he was walking in the middle of nowhere and he thought I wanted something from him. I suppose folks are just naturally suspicious these days, but still and all… "No sir. I thought maybe I could do something for you. I'm headed into town and thought maybe I could give you a lift."

That old man lowered his head for just a second, as though gathering his thoughts, then slowly raised it again. A slow smile formed inside that beard of his and his shoulders visibly sagged in relief as though he could no longer hide his tiredness. "That would be right nice. Thank you very much."

I unlocked the passenger side door and waited while he opened it, climbed on in and got settled next to me. He dropped his bag on the floor between his feet, buckled up, and sighed, relaxing against the back of the seat as though it was the most comfortable thing he'd ever sat on. I smiled as I watched. I'd been there many a time after a long day. I glanced at the road and then back at him. "All set?"

He nodded "Yup."

I motioned with my right hand towards the still open door. "Can't really go anywheres until that thing is closed."

He laughed, a slow kind of rumble from deep in his chest. "Ah… right. Guess I forgot. Not much used to traveling in these kind of things anymore."

Grieco

The door gave a satisfying thud as he closed it… the kind of sound you don't get with the newer models. I looked in the rear view to see if there was anything coming, … there wasn't… should of known that… not much traffic along this stretch of road anymore… leastwise since the mill closed down… nonetheless, it never hurts to be sure…, and then slowly pulled back out onto the road headed towards town.

Don't get much chance at conversation with strangers round here, so it wasn't too long before I felt compelled to ask, "Been walking long?" Seemed like as good a way as any to start things off.

That old man pulled his Santa hat off his head and rubbed the top of his head, ruffling up hair that grew sparser the higher up it got. "Long enough. Didn't think anyone would ever come along. Thought I'd have to walk all the way to the hospital."

That got my attention. "You sick or something? Do I need to get you there in a hurry?"

He laughed again; a rich burble of sound that made me want to laugh along. "No… I'm not sick. I'm headed there to bring some cheer to the folks who'll be spending Christmas there."

I shook my head, just a little, as I eyed the empty bag between his feet. "Uh… were you planning on giving folks…" I trailed off and gave a little nod towards his bag.

His eyes dropped to the floorboard, and he pushed the bag with his feet. "Oh you mean the bag. It looks empty, doesn't it?"

"Ah, yeah."

Little Book of Stories

He picked that bag up and rolled it around in his hands for a moment before dropping it back between his feet. "Well it is. Now."

"Now?"

"Yup. There'll be more than enough to go around once I get started."

"You mean the gifts are already at the hospital."

"Something like that."

The car got quiet except for some road noise and the occasional screech of wipers clearing away the spatter of wet stuff that mixed with the blowing snow. After a bit, that old man started fiddling with something he had attached to his belt. It was a little silver cylinder, about the size of a large saltshaker. Had all sorts of symbols and pictographs all over it from what I could see. 'Course, I couldn't tell for sure since I had to keep most of my attention on the road. Still in all, what with all that fidgeting and fiddling, I couldn't help but wonder what that silver thing was. Finally, I just had to ask.

"So what the heck is that thing you seem so preoccupied with?"

That old man looked up with a little look of surprise on his face, like he'd been caught doing something he really shouldn't of been doing. "What?"

"That silver thing you're messing with... What is it?"

Well, he got a kind of soft smile that seemed to start from nowhere in particular and spread until it filled his whole face. He unhooked the cylinder from his belt and held it up so I could get a better look. "This... silver thing as you call it is what makes my sleigh run."

Grieco

Now I've heard of some Santas building up entire stories around their time in the suit. One guy claimed that he had a second workshop in Buenos Aries. He had this real thick Hispanic accent and used this tale to explain why he spoke Spanish so well. Another one said he treated his reindeer to vacations in Tahiti as a way of explaining his deep dark tan. But, I had to admit, the silver cylinder routine was something new. I had to know more.

"That thing there makes your sled run?"

"Yep..."

"OK. I'll bite. What do you call it?"

"What do you mean?"

"You know... everything has a name of some sort. Cars have carburetors and spark plugs and tires and all sorts of things they need to let them run. Everything has a name... even that thing." I nodded my head towards the cylinder in his hand.

That old man looked at the cylinder as though it was the first time he'd ever seen it. He moved it around, looking at it from all angles as though doing so would reveal something he hadn't seen before. "You know... I've never really thought about it before. I guess you might think of it as something like a spark plug. 'Cept instead of just providing a spark to get things going, it holds all the energy needed to get the sleigh up and off the ground so the reindeer can pull it through the sky."

"That little thing holds enough energy to move your sled?" I didn't mean to sound skeptical. After all, I was just getting the details of this guy's Santa story. Still and all, some level of doubt must of shown in my response. He just threw back his head and laughed a laugh that seemed to come from deep in his belly and, maybe it was just my imagination, kinda shook the entire truck in a buzzy, vibrational sort of way.

As his laughter slowly faded, the truck seemed somewhat dimmer, as though a light had gone out somewhere close by. He sat there for a moment with a thoughtful look on his face as though reaching for a word that just wouldn't come. Then he seemed to give up and glanced over at me. "What would you call something that captures and stores good will and cheer and then acts like a battery, releasing what's stored to power the sleigh?"

I thought about it for a minute before replying. "Cheerinator?" Even to me it sounded kinda silly, like something from a Schwarzenegger movie, but that old man just nodded to himself as though it was the best name anyone ever came up with.

"Cheerinator..." He nodded again. "I like it. It fits." He held up the cylinder again. "Well this... Cheerinator measures and captures all the good will and cheer it detects as we pass by. Then it feeds it to the sleigh's... motivator I guess you'd call it. Acts like a sort of anti-grav device that lets the sleigh float in the air, allowing it to escape gravity and fly where I need to go."

I nodded at the cylinder. "That little thing does all that?"

He laughed again, softer this time. "Yep. It's the heart and soul of the sleigh. In fact it's why I was walking when you stopped to pick me up."

"How so?"

"Well... the cheerinator captures all the... energy... yes that's it... energy generated by folks good will and cheer. Normally it's pretty abundant this time of year and the cheerinator captures more than enough to keep the sleigh up and going. Even when we hit a patch where things are tough and folks don't feel all that cheerful, it still usually has enough to carry us through until we get to a spot where folks are feeling better."

This time I nodded. I was enjoying this guy's ability to build a story on the fly, especially one that looked like it was going to hold together. Still… "So if that's true, how did you end up on the road back there?"

That old man looked down at his boots, seemingly embarrassed at having been caught up short by what looked to me to be a hole in his story. Then he looked up again, smiled a little ruefully and said, "Well… times are tougher in some areas than in others."

I nodded again and motioned with my hand for him to go on.

"When I hit a spot where times are really tough, the cheerinator seems to drain faster than in other places. Almost as though it's trying to release some of that cheer into the wind to filter down and make up some of the difference." He looked over at me, "I think you know things are tougher than usual around here…"

I nodded once more, aware of how the mill closure and jobs moving away had pretty well destroyed any good cheer that might have existed for this season. Folks were trying to scrape by any which way they could, never mind gather themselves up for a holiday they couldn't afford and didn't much feel like celebrating.

That old man could tell from my expression that I knew exactly what he was talking about. After all, all I had for the orphanage was a bunch of Dollar Store items masquerading as presents for the kids. I settled deeper into the seat as reality set in. I'd managed to forget about it for awhile talking to a fella Santa, but now it hit home all over again.

Little Book of Stories

Taking my silence as his cue to keep talking, he continued. "The empty space around here was just so big that this cheerinator just ran out of energy before we could get across. The sleigh just sort of sputtered out. Fortunately, there's always a little residue left over so we don't just fall out of the sky. But we were well and truly stuck, don't you know.

We came down a little distance away from the road I was walking on when you picked me up. The cheerinator doesn't run out of juice very often mind you. But when it does, I always try to land far enough away from the road so that nobody will find my sleigh while I'm off trying to find some way to recharge it. Lucky thing you happened by. I would have had to walk all the way to the hospital if you hadn't. I don't mind telling you that with the wind and all, I was feeling a mite chilly out there."

He stopped then, almost as though he'd run out of words. But that was alright, I was still feeling pretty low, even with his company and tall tales about sleighs and that cheerinator thing. But then it hit me, he'd mentioned the hospital again. I glanced at him real quick, making sure that I didn't take my eyes off the road for too long. After all, you never know when you might run up against a stretch of ice or maybe some drifting snow that was just kinda hiding around a curve in the road. "You sure you're alright? Not too many folks would want to go to the hospital in weather like this unless they had a good reason."

He laughed again. That slow rumble coming from someplace deep inside his chest seemed to make the dashboard hum and vibrate in tune with the sound. "Oh, I've got a good reason. There's a whole lot of folks there that just might need some good cheer, kids especially. Nobody should miss Christmas just because they're stuck in some antiseptic ward away from home and family." He gave me a sidelong look, a small smile set on his face as though he was just barely succeeding at trying not to laugh again. "I'd think you'd agree that Santa should always go where he's needed, especially on a night like this."

He had me with that and somehow, I found myself smiling despite the gloom that I'd felt just a moment before. Yep. Here we were. Two Santas out to make the world just a little bit better than it might otherwise be. We fell into an easy silence then. The kind that old friends might have when they'd said all that needed to be said and simple companionship was all that was called for. I don't know why it felt that way. I'd only picked him up a short time before, but somehow it seemed like I'd known him my whole life. We drove on that way until we reached the hospital, me staring through the windshield at the blowing snow and him just watching the snow-covered scenery as it passed on by.

The hospital parking lot was pretty much empty 'cause of the snow. What with the snow piling up and the sky continuing to spew more, I pulled up as close as I could get to the entrance. It was only after we'd parked that it occurred to me that it would be pretty strange for two Santas to show up. It'd probably just confuse the kids and anyone else who happened to be in the building. So I just sat there, hands still on the wheel, while I tried to sort through what to do. After a moment or two, that old timer gave me a look that said he knew something was up.

"Something the matter, young fella?"

I paused, still trying to figure out what I felt about what I was about to suggest. After all, I'd been looking forward to giving out gifts probably as much as the kids were to having Santa visit. "No. ... Not really."

That old man gave me a knowing look but waited in silence, not saying anything else. Finally, he asked, "Aren't you going in?"

I turned and looked at him, dressed in that red suit, hair and beard white as snow, empty sack at his feet. He looked more like Santa than I ever had, than I ever would, even with my Santa suit and pillows and fake beard. My voice didn't sound real to me even as I said the words. "I think you should do it."

"Do what?"

"I think you should be Santa for the kids this year."

That old man frowned then, the first time I'd seen anything that didn't resemble a smile on his face. "Why I couldn't. You've obviously been looking forward to this. Planned the whole thing." He glanced at the back seat where my bag of Dollar Store gifts was stashed. "And from the looks of things, you've probably even paid for presents for the kids out of your own pocket."

My head dropped towards my chest. He was right. I was looking forward to this. It would have been the bright spot in a sad, long year for me as much as for the kids. I lifted my head and looked him straight in the eye, "You're right. I was… and I did." I motioned towards my bag in the back seat. "But somehow, I suspect you're ten times the Santa than I'll ever be… and what I want more than anything is for the kids in that hospital over there to have a good Christmas, a bit of joy and happiness in their lives, … and unless I'm very much mistaken, you seem tailor made for the job."

He gazed at me with eyes that seemed as old as time itself and then nodded, as though to himself. "Are you sure about this?"

Grieco

I paused for just a moment, searching within myself for the answer. Then I nodded in return. "Yes. I think you should do it ... be Santa for the kids this year."

His frown lessened, then disappeared as the smile returned to his face. "Well, I can't do it alone young man. I'll need you to be my helper... if you don't mind playing second fiddle to an old codger like me."

I found myself smiling in return, somehow certain that I'd made the right decision. "I'd be delighted to help."

"Well then, let's be on with it, shall we?"

Santa, ... I figured I might as well call him Santa. After all, old timer just didn't seem right, and he was just about to play the part. ... Santa pulled his cap back on his head and adjusted it, clipped that cheerinator thing back on his belt, grabbed the empty bag from the floorboards between his feet, and then opened the door to practically spring out of my car. I opened my mouth to warn him about ice on the pavement. They never really clean the parking lot real good until at least a day or two after a storm. But he was steady as a rock, standing there waiting for me to get a move on.

I started to grab my Santa suit, but my fingers stopped just short of touching it as I remembered I wouldn't be needing it after all. I sat there for just a moment, regret washing over me. The urge to put on that suit was so strong that I almost changed my mind right there and then. Didn't realize I'd miss doing it so much. Didn't realize how much I needed it, maybe more than the kids waiting inside for Santa to appear. But no, ... I'd already promised that old timer... Santa... that he'd be the one bringing smiles to those faces this year. My hand slowly pulled back and I grabbed the door handle instead. I opened my door and, much more gingerly, did my best to get out without making a fool of myself by slipping and sliding and falling flat on my keister. I managed, after a fashion, holding on to the roof rack for support as I moved to the back door, opened it, and carefully lifted out my bag with the gifts. Then, bag in hand, I moved carefully to join that old… Santa where he stood, patiently, a small smile forming as he watched my antics.

"You've got to be careful there." Santa cautioned me. "This ice is a mite slippery."

My astonishment must have shown on my face for he continued. "My boots have special soles, designed specifically to grip in conditions like these. I'd have to try real hard to slip walking on this stuff. Here, take my hand. I think I have enough traction to get us to the entrance."

Nobody wants to admit that they can't make it a couple of hundred feet across a parking lot without falling down. But… I did have that bag, and it'd be a shame if those Dollar Store gifts got smashed because I was too proud to take a helping hand. I grabbed that old man's… Santa's hand and moved the last few feet to where he stood. Funny thing, as soon as I took his hand, I felt steadier, more sure on my feet. I know it was just my imagination, but when we started across that parking lot, I didn't slip once. Didn't even feel my feet slide on any of that ice and snow between us and the door. Wasn't too long before we were safe and sound, inside the building and on our way to the reception area.

The hospital was pretty deserted. Most non-essential folks had been released when the storm had started moving in. Those that were there were surprised to see me. I guess they hadn't really expected anyone to come out on a day like this. Still, their faces lit up at the sight of my bag, their eyes growing wide at the sight of Santa walking by my side. And that old man, why he went into full Santa mode the moment he saw their eyes on him. He let out a huge laugh that shock the entire reception area, followed a moment later by a loud "Ho, Ho, Ho" that even I had to smile at. The very sound of his voice seemed to make the whole room brighter, more full of light. I found myself trailing along in his wake as he greeted each staff member by name, reaching into his bag to pull out some small trinket that seemed to be just what that person needed to make their day just a bit better.

Some folks might think it remarkable that he was able to greet each one by name. But I knew better. That's an old trick, used by every Santa who ever worked an office party. Just look at the person's nametag as you come up to them and then act like you knew it all along. You'd be surprised how many people never even stop to think about that. They're just so pleased to have Santa know their name, to have that little bit of recognition.

'Course this guy seemed to know their names even when their nametags were covered by a bit of sweater or a lab coat. Impressive, I had to admit. He never seemed to skip a beat. But then, I knew that trick too. You just hesitate, just a second or so, "and this is…", and most folks will happily volunteer their name to fill in the empty space. Then Santa just has to nod wisely and smile and repeat the name as though he knew it all along. This old man though, he didn't seem to pause for even a second as he moved from person to person, smiling and laughing and poking gentle fun at this or that. And each time he stopped, he reached into that empty bag only to find that it wasn't quite so empty after all, that there was just one more gift to be found and given out.

I don't know how he did it. Must be some sort of magic trick, some sleight of hand that he'd figured out over long years of doing this. Whatever it was, I'd definitely have to get him to show it to me after we finished making the rounds.

Then, as quick as it had started, he "Ho, Ho, Hoed" once again, said his goodbyes, and wished them "A Merry Christmas to all!". He looked to me with a raised eyebrow and mouthed the words "The kids?". I nodded in understanding and asked a nearby nurse if they could take us up to the children's ward. She, still caught up in Santa's spell and charmed by his constant banter, quickly agreed, and led us off to an elevator. It wasn't long before we were exiting on the fifth floor into a broad open area where cushions, bean bags chairs, low slung tables, and kid-sized chairs were haphazardly arranged. A small assortment of plush animals was scattered around the area as though abandoned in mid play. A small fake fir tree was off in one corner of the room, its twinkling lights randomly illuminating the tinsel and shiny ornaments adorning it.

Perhaps spurred by the sound of the elevator doors closing, the face of a young girl, no more than five, peered around the corner of a doorway at the opposite end of the room. Her solemn expression instantly changed to one of amazement and then to joy at the sight of the old man in the red suit. "Santa!" She cried, looking behind her at something we could not see. "Santa is here!" And with that, she came around the corner with all the speed she could muster, left leg encased in an enormous cast, body swinging in time with the movement of the crutches that supported her weight. It wasn't long before a flood of children swarmed through the doorway, accompanied by several nurses and other staff who assisted those unable to move without help. They eagerly moved up to Santa, surrounding him and trying to get as close as they could, with several hugging him and holding on as though they'd never let go. All the while, that old man laughed, his belly jiggling and moving as though it had a mind of its own.

Finally, the nurses gently pried the children off Santa and led him to a chair that one of them had set up near the tree while the children were clamoring for his attention.

Then the real magic began. I say magic, for I have no idea how he did it. One by one, the kids were brought up to him. Some were shy. Some were downright anxious to jump in his lap or hug and hold him. Santa welcomed each and every one with a smile, sharing some secret Christmas message that seemed tailor made for each child. Then he'd reach into that bag of his and pull out a toy, or book, or stuffed animal to give to the child. No one was disappointed. Each child seemed to get just what they wanted, or as close to it that it made no difference either way. After visiting with Santa, each one would move, as if by agreement, to a different part of the room to sit with the gift they had just received. Eventually, after the last of the kids had chatted with Santa, received their gifts, and moved away, he rose from the chair to talk briefly with each of the staff, again pulling some item from his bag to give to each of them.

It was then that I saw it. That cheerinator thing on his belt was glowing, giving off a silvery light. I'd thought I'd noticed it earlier, slowly growing brighter with each gift given, each laugh heard, each shout of joy, and each smile that sprang up on the faces of the staff and children, but I figured it was just my imagination. But there was no way I could miss that glow now. No one else seemed to see it, but it was as clear to me as the sun at mid-day, shining with a light so bright that I almost had to look away. That old man caught me staring but only smiled, a broad secret smile that only I would understand, and shifted the cheerinator on his belt so that it was covered by a fold of his suit and some fringe. All the while, he continued to chat and make small talk, until he'd visited at least once with every person, child or staff, in the room.

And then, just like that, it was over. That old man moved through the room, gently but surely disengaging until he was back by the elevator. He motioned for me to join him, and without a second thought, I did. When the doors opened, we entered. He backed in, smiling and waving all the while. With one last "Merry Christmas!" the doors closed, and, with a press of a button, we were on our way to the ground floor. As the elevator moved downward, he gave me a wisp of smile, somehow somewhat sad, as though he'd used up some reservoir of strength he'd saved for the visit with the kids. He seemed to sag a bit, still every bit Santa, but somehow smaller. He looked at me, his face a mix of joy and regret. "I guess it's time to go." he said as the elevator came to a stop and the doors opened.

There were still staff around as we walked back into the reception area. That old man immediately sprang back into Santa mode, laughing and joking as we made our way to the exit and back into the cold, and blowing snow. We stood there for a few moments, under the lights of the hospital entrance, watching the snow swirl and settle as the wind caught it and blew it across the parking lot. I shivered as the cold snuck under the seams of my coat.

As I moved to zip it more fully up, I realized that I was still holding my Santa bag in one hand, somehow having completely forgotten it in my wonder at watching the old man go through his paces. He gave me a knowing, sympathetic glance. "Never mind. Save those gifts for next year. It'll give you a head start." He paused before continuing. "Thank you for letting me be Santa to the kids and staff. I can only imagine how much you were looking forward to it, how important it was to you to be here today."

I felt a twinge, a spark of regret, but it was gone in an instant. It was my turn to smile as I replied. "You know, I thought I'd be sad at not being Santa, at missing this year." I gestured vaguely back at the hospital. "But I'm not. All I really wanted to do was bring some happiness to the kids back there, to brighten up their lives and bring them some joy." I placed my free hand on his arm. "I guess I have to thank you. You managed to do everything I wanted to, and more. If, in the future, I can do half of what you did today, I'll be satisfied." I looked back out at the snow and wind. "I don't know where you're headed now, but if you need one, I'd be happy to give you a lift."

The smile that crossed his face almost made me forget the weather. "Why thank you. A ride would be right nice about now." He offered me his hand. "Hold on to me. I don't suppose that pavement has gotten any less slippery since we've been here."

We crossed the parking lot cautiously; my feet tending to slip and slide while that old man just seemed as steady as a rock. He took care to keep me upright, never faltering even when he had to support me to keep me from falling. We finally made it to my car and, after stashing my bag behind the front seat, we climbed in and shut the doors as quickly as we could manage. When he dropped his bag on the floor between his feet, it still looked as empty as the first time I saw it.

I couldn't help but sigh. "I've just got to ask." I began. He just looked at me, as though waiting for the question he'd been expecting all day. "That bag of your is empty, been empty all day, and yet you kept pulling gifts out of it. … I've seen some magic acts in my day, but that… your bag routine, that is something I just can't explain. How'd you do it? How does it work?"

He looked from me to his bag and then back again. "Ah… I'm afraid that's a trade secret. It is magic, of course, after a sort. But I hope you understand that I can't reveal what makes it work."

I nodded. I'd kind of expected an answer like this, but, still, I'd hoped to get some sort of insight into the magic bag thing. "I do understand. I just hoped…"

He looked at me, the sympathy clear in his expression. "I can't tell you how it works, but I can tell you this. There's always something there when I reach inside. The bag somehow seems to attune itself to the person I'm visiting with. Whether it's something small or somewhat bigger, the item that comes out is always just right."

I nodded again, not really satisfied with the answer but figuring that I wasn't going to get anything better. I fastened my seatbelt, waited for him to do the same, then started the car and slowly moved across the parking lot and back onto the road. I glanced over at him, being careful not to take my eyes off the road for too long. "Headed anywhere in particular? Someplace I can drop you off at?"

That old man sank back into the seat, his head laying back against the rest, eyes half closed as he relaxed. "No. No place in particular. If you could drop me off near where you picked me up, I'd appreciate it. As I told you earlier, I left my sleigh near there. Need to get back and be on my way."

I couldn't help but smile. He was clearly determined not to drop out of character even now, after we'd finished with our visit to the hospital. I had to respect that from a fellow Santa, so I thought I'd play along. "Right… your sleigh. I guess I forgot about that." I glanced over at him. "Don't you still need to charge up that cheerinator? If I remember right, you said it was necessary to make the sleigh run."

He reached down and unhooked the cheerinator from his belt and held it up as though examining it. "Got a good charge back there at the hospital. … Funny thing about making people happy. … They give off just the right kind of energy this thing needs to operate." He rubbed the cylinder on his suit as though polishing it up. As he hooked it back onto his belt, I could swear that sucker gleamed and gave off a soft white light. I know that I was only imagining it, but still… that old man had me reeled in, completely hooked.

We rode on, after that, in companionable silence, the only sound being the windblown snow hitting the windshield and the sound of the wipers doing their best to keep that stuff from piling up. Ever so often, I had to roll down the window and reach my hand around to pull off some of the buildup so I could see the road. Consequently, I was startled when he final spoke.

"This will do. You can drop me off anywhere here."

I slowed the car and carefully came to a stop. Didn't bother to pull over. Nobody else was going to be on the road at this point. "You sure? There's nothing out here."

"'Cept my sleigh."

Yeah, his sleigh. I respect someone spinning their Santa story to the bitter end, but this, this was taking things way too far. I turned to him, my face clearly showing my concern. "You can't be serious. I mean… this is in the middle of nowhere. You'll freeze to death in no time in this weather."

His face turned serious. "You're not buying the sleigh thing, huh?"

I shook my head. "No. I'm not. And from one Santa to another, I'm not going to let you go out there in the snow unless I know you've got someplace to go that's warm and dry."

He placed his thumb against the side of his nose and gave me a conspiratorial look. "Well ok then. From one Santa to another, what if I told you that my sleigh was really a well-equipped RV with heat and water and a well-stocked fridge with a whole stack of frozen dinners just waiting for me to fire up the microwave?"

I paused, unsure whether to believe him. "So, where is this RV?"

He peered through the front window, then pointed at a turnoff almost obscured by snowdrifts. "It's just down that dirt road. I parked it there when the storm started coming in. Didn't want to get caught trying to drive that thing on roads like this."

I sat back some, almost believing him. "An RV huh?"

"Yep."

"That Santa's base of operations?"

He smiled then and any misgivings I still had somehow disappeared. "Yep. I drive around the country in that thing and set up near places where they could use a bit of holiday cheer. Everybody's happy to see Santa. I'd like to think that I've made the world a slightly better place by the time I've left. Leastwise I hope I have. ... Want to see my setup? It's just a hundred feet or so over there."

I looked at the drifts building at the entrance to the turnoff and then back at the road ahead. It didn't look like the snow was going to stop any time soon. If I stopped now to try to drive to his RV, I was probably going to be stuck there for the night at least. That wouldn't do. I had to get back. The wife would be worried, and I still needed to play Santa for my kids. No. There came a time when you just had to trust a body. If that old man told me he had an RV just down there a bit, I was going to have to believe him.

"No. That's ok. I have to get home. … But you sure you're going to be alright?"

He nodded his head, a broad smile stretching his face near to breaking. "I'll be fine." He started to reach for the door handle, then stopped as though he'd just remembered something. He reached down and picked up his bag, stuck one hand deep inside and rummaged around for a moment. "Ah… here it is." He dropped the bag back on the floor and turned to me, his hand holding something that he held out for me to take. "Here. This is for you."

I hesitated, but he gestured again, gently waving the object. "Come on Bill, take it. From one Santa to another at Christmas."

Well, that did it. When he put it that way, I couldn't say no. I reached out and took it, mumbling my thanks. Then I looked at it. "Wait. This is a five-hundred-dollar gas card. I can't accept this. It's too much."

He frowned, almost looking confused for just a moment. "Is it? Huh… I never really know what I'm going to get when I reach in the bag. That's part of the magic. But it wouldn't have given me that card if it wasn't meant for you."

"But…" I began, still holding the card out towards him.

He smiled again. "Humor this old man, Bill. Certainly you could use that card?"

I looked at him, then at the card, and slowly tucked the card away in my coat pocket. He was right. That card would go a long way towards paying for the gas I'd use between work and helping less fortunate folks around town. "Thank you." was all I could muster. It sounded inadequate even to me, but sometimes a thanks is all you have when someone does something nice like that for you.

He nodded and reached for the doorhandle, opening it, and moving on out into the snow and wind. "You are most welcome Bill. Say hi to the wife and kids for me... and Merry Christmas!"

"Wait!" I said, as he went to close the door. "Aren't you going to take your bag?"

He looked momentarily surprised, as though he'd forgotten all about it. Then he bent under the doorframe, and laughed, a soft, low rumbling sound. "Ah, ... no Bill. You keep it. That's one of my spares. I've got dozens of them at home and a few more in the RV." He smiled as he moved to straighten up. "You might find it handy come next Christmas. It'll work for you just as well as it did for me. ... You'll see" Then he shut the door and moved away into the storm.

I waited and watched while he crossed the road, head bowed against the blowing snow. He turned and waved once he reached the turnoff, then trudged up the dirt road to vanish in the white, swirling stuff. I sat a moment longer, hand still on the pocket holding the gas card. Then I reached over and picked up the bag he'd left behind. Empty. Just like I'd thought. But it'd been empty the whole time he'd been giving out gifts at the hospital. I knew better than to believe any of the stories of Santa and magic and all that other stuff. After all, I played Santa and there certainly was no magic in me. But still... I carefully folded that bag and placed it, with care, on the now empty passenger seat next to me.

I had just started to put the car in gear when a flash from somewhere down the turnoff road caught my attention. It was a bright light, penetrating through the storm and illuminating, for just a moment, the trees, road, and snow. I almost thought I caught a glimpse of something red rising into the sky as the light faded and the winter dark reclaimed everything.

Nah. It couldn't be. My mind was just playing tricks on me, making me see what I wanted to see, what I hoped to see on a night like this. I put the car in gear and started going, very slowly, down the road. Being careful to avoid the drifts, I focused entirely on keeping the car out of a ditch or sliding, out of control, across some hidden patch of ice. I was a mile or so from home when it occurred to me that I'd never told that old man my name. Hadn't told him I was married or that I had kids. Shoot, we'd hadn't talked about much at all, except Santa stuff and the kids at the hospital. So how did he...? Someone at the hospital had to have told him. That's it. It had to be it. He couldn't have been...

I was still thinking about it when I finally pulled the car into the driveway, put it in park, turned off the lights and then the engine. I put my hand into my pocket and felt for the gas card, just to make certain it was real, to make sure that that old man hadn't been just a figment of my imagination. I felt the hard contours of the card with my fingers, then looked at the bag the old man had pulled it from.

"It looks empty, doesn't it?" His words sounded loud in my head, almost as though he was still in the car with me. I shook my head and laughed at my foolishness. But still, I reached over and gathered up that bag, carrying it carefully as I made my way to my front door. Who knows. It just might come in handy someday, ... maybe tonight...

The night before...

"Honest officer, it all happened so fast... I'm not sure I can describe it...What? Alright, I'll try.

We were fast asleep, I in my kerchief and Pa in his cap, when it happened.

Suddenly we heard this huge noise. It sounded like it was on the lawn at first. Pa got up grumbling about how some folks have no respect for decent folks just trying to get some sleep. Figured it was the neighborhood kids, a bunch of hooligans that's what they are.

Well Pa went to the window and pulled up the blinds, just to check things out don't you know.

You know how it snowed the other day? Well, it was laying white and thick out there on the lawn and Pa figured he'd sure 'nuf catch them hooligans traipsing around out there hip deep in all that snow.

Yep. He'd catch 'em red handed and take names so he could call their parents and wake them up from a sound sleep and see how they'd like it.

Funny thing though. When he looked out the window, there weren't nobody there... just the front yard covered in snow. Pa lifted up his cap, scratched at his head for just a bit, shrugged, and turned 'round to get back in bed.

But before he could even take half a step there was this sound of bells a jingling and a ringing to beat the band. Pa turned right back around, and this time opened that window and stuck his head right out.

He says he saw some sort of sleigh with reindeer and stuff, but I think that was the eggnog talking. Pa does love to spike his nog... He uses the good stuff... None of that cheap booze for his nog. No sirree.

Well anyways, the next thing we know there's this loud noise up on the roof like a thousand hooves all a clattering and a clacking. Frightened the heck out of us.

Well Pa went right for his gun. ... Keeps it in the nightstand drawer right over there by the bed. ... After he'd got it, we just stood there and listened to try and figure out what was going on.

Then we heard a noise in the living room... a loud thump like something had fallen down the chimney. Well we crept out into the hallway silent as church mice. ... After all, we had no idea what was going on. ... Went right over to the banister and peeked on down to where we had the tree and all our presents, just waiting for morning.

Pa made a small noise, sucked in his breath, and raised his gun. There was somebody down there!

Pa slowly reached for the light switch with his other hand and clicked it on. There, standing like a deer in the headlights, was this fella all dressed in red and fur, dirty and covered in soot, with a bag at his feet and one hand stuck deep inside like he was putting something in it.

Well it was pretty clear that we was being robbed. That cheeky fella had somehow squirmed his way down the chimney and was in the middle of stealing all our presents. Scandalous... that's what it was.

Well that fella took one look at us and started to shake, kinda like a bowl of jelly, and started to make a low rumbling sound one might have mistaken for laughter ifn the situation been different.

But Pa weren't having none of that. He steadied his gun…
after all, that nog was a mite strong and his hand was
shaking just a bit from the excitement… and that fella stood
up and looked him right in the eye.

Pa swore later that that fella started to reach for
something… although it looked to me like he was trying to
decide what do.

Maybe it was all that shaking that did it, but BLAM! Pa's
gun just went off. … Hit the mantle about a foot from the
fella. … Never really got close to hitting him, but just like
that there was some sort of cloud of soot and ash and that
fella had just up and disappeared.

Pa dropped the gun right there on the landing. I think he
was more surprised than anything else. … Don't think he
really intended to shoot… more of a threat than anything
else… but it did the trick.

Well, it was only a minute or so later that we heard that
clatter again up there on the roof and some sort of loud
shout… probably that fella yelling to his accomplices.

We ran back to the bedroom and Pa stuck his head out the
window to see if he could get a better look at whoever that
fella was…

Must've hit his head real hard when he pulled it back in,
'cause he started babbling about a sleigh and tiny reindeer
flying through the sky. … Swore he saw it as clear as I see
you now.

Personally, I think it was the nog and the shock from the
burglary. Ain't no such thing as flying reindeer. Still and
all, Pa says we're gonna call some folks about putting a
grating over the chimney top.

Grieco

Can't say I blame him. I know I'll sleep better once we get that thing put on. Just never know what might try and come down.

It all happened so fast officer. I'm not sure I told it all... What? That's all you need?

You sure? Well okay then. Thanks for coming by.

Yeah.

Merry Christmas to you too."

The Beggar and The King

Once, not so very long ago, there lived a mighty King. The King was quite wealthy as his lands were vast and his vassals and subjects paid their taxes dutifully, if reluctantly.

His vassals owed their lands, their livelihoods, and their lives to his favor. Thus, throughout the kingdom, they enforced his laws, kept the King's peace, and paid heed to his every whim and desire. Each year at Christmas, the King would summon them to come and renew their allegiance. Being unable to refuse, these nobles would leave their lands and travel to the palace of the King where there would be great ceremony, pageantry, and offering of gifts.

With all his vassals gathered near, the King would give a great feast at Christmas for these noble folk. Food and drink were plentiful, with each course of the meal being more fabulous than the one before. Throughout the feast, long into the night, the palace walls resounded with song and the practiced laughter of the powerful as they competed to keep or gain the favor of the King.

Also in the kingdom, indeed not so very far from the walls of the King's palace, there lived a beggar. With rags for clothes, he would seek to gain a living, day after day, from the cast offs and refuse of others. It was a hard life, yet he somehow managed to provide just enough for him and his family to survive.

Each year at Christmas, the beggar also traveled to the King's palace. Once there, he would stand among a crowd gazing hopefully at the procession of finely dressed lords and ladies on their way to the King's feast. As they passed the gathered folk, a few of those nobles would toss coins to those assembled there. And as the coins fell to the cobbled streets, the beggar would scramble with all the rest to grab as many as possible before the procession moved on. For, having given alms to the gathered poor, the nobles would hurry on to the feast awaiting them.

As evening fell, the beggar would make his way homeward. As he went, he would gather bread and meat cast away by the King's servants as they prepared the Christmas feast. Thus it was that, by the time the beggar reached his hut, he had more than enough food for himself and his family. Seeing this, he would go round and invite his friends, who were as poor as he, to share in his good fortune. As friends do, each would bring something of their own to contribute to the Christmas meal. And so, each year, they drew together around a meal more wonderful than any could remember for a long, long time. The beggar sang and laughed with his friends and all were joined by the love that filled the hut.

And so two feasts took place on Christmas. Tell me, which man was richer that day: the beggar, or the King?

Grieco

Grieco

There are none so blind
as those who say they see
and understand
when they do not.

For there is certainty
in ignorance,
and from certainty
does action come,
and it is in action
that our ends
become manifest.

Grieco

ABOUT THE AUTHOR

Born and raised in a small rural town, the author left to pursue higher education and a career which took him to different parts of the world. After a lifetime listening to the whisper of the wind, the burble of a brook, and the sound of songbirds all imparting their wisdom, he's returned to his roots, spending his days as a country gentleman, taking the time now and then to put some words on paper.

You can find more from the author at pat-grieco.com